RAVENHEART

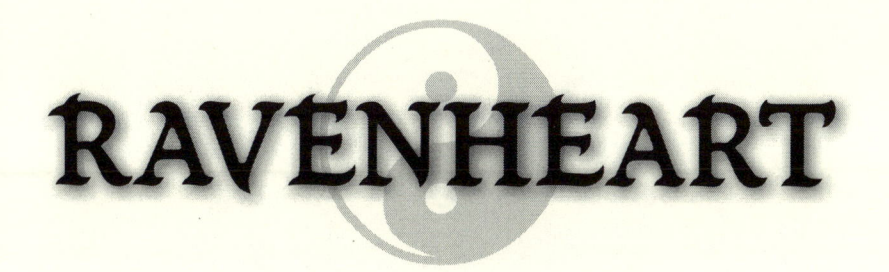

BOOK 1

*To Ken + Holly,
With thanks for
all you do,
— Melissa*

MELISSA J. JOHNSON

BALBOA PRESS
A DIVISION OF HAY HOUSE

Copyright © 2018 Melissa J. Johnson.

All rights reserved. No part of this book may be used or reproduced by any means, graphic, electronic, or mechanical, including photocopying, recording, taping or by any information storage retrieval system without the written permission of the author except in the case of brief quotations embodied in critical articles and reviews.

This is a work of fiction. All of the characters, names, incidents, organizations, and dialogue in this novel are either the products of the author's imagination or are used fictitiously.

Balboa Press books may be ordered through booksellers or by contacting:

Balboa Press
A Division of Hay House
1663 Liberty Drive
Bloomington, IN 47403
www.balboapress.com
1 (877) 407-4847

Because of the dynamic nature of the Internet, any web addresses or links contained in this book may have changed since publication and may no longer be valid. The views expressed in this work are solely those of the author and do not necessarily reflect the views of the publisher, and the publisher hereby disclaims any responsibility for them.

The author of this book does not dispense medical advice or prescribe the use of any technique as a form of treatment for physical, emotional, or medical problems without the advice of a physician, either directly or indirectly. The intent of the author is only to offer information of a general nature to help you in your quest for emotional and spiritual well-being. In the event you use any of the information in this book for yourself, which is your constitutional right, the author and the publisher assume no responsibility for your actions.

Any people depicted in stock imagery provided by Getty Images are models, and such images are being used for illustrative purposes only. Certain stock imagery © Getty Images.

Print information available on the last page.

ISBN: 978-1-9822-1209-4 (sc)
ISBN: 978-1-9822-1207-0 (hc)
ISBN: 978-1-9822-1208-7 (e)

Library of Congress Control Number: 2018910849

Balboa Press rev. date: 09/17/2018

CONTENTS

Chapter 1	Loss	1
Chapter 2	The Cave	9
Chapter 3	A Tale of Two Women	17
Chapter 4	The Tale Continues	31
Chapter 5	Meeting Dougal	40
Chapter 6	The Witch's Ride	45
Chapter 7	A Call from a Queen	49
Chapter 8	Murray	56
Chapter 9	Liu (Lou) Shen	63
Chapter 10	Magic	77
Chapter 11	The Slig Maith	88
Chapter 12	The Prince	102
Chapter 13	Bernadette and the Queen	110
Chapter 14	Lost	124
Chapter 15	Forresgem	130
Chapter 16	The Kirk	138
Chapter 17	The Sheriff	148
Chapter 18	A Meeting	163
Chapter 19	A Journey	174
Chapter 20	In the Dark	187
Chapter 21	Revenge	195
Chapter 22	Wanting	203
Chapter 23	Flight	208

1

LOSS

My mum had just served a thick vegetable stew. She, my little sister, and I ate the whole thing. As I sat on the dirt floor of our croft, wiping out the bowls with fistfuls of grass, Mum sat next to the light of the fire, putting small bags of herbs together. Some of the herbs we grew in our garden; others we gathered on the sly in the laird's forest. We were not supposed to do that, but Mum said he wouldn't miss them. She gathered catnip, bergamot, nettles, and sometimes mushrooms. In our garden, we had roses, thyme, rosemary, and other herbs. She made bags of dried herbs for digestion, sleeplessness, bowel movements, and other healing necessities. I was humming a tune I'd recently heard at a neighbor's croft, and the room smelled of stew and the pungent herbs Mum worked with.

Suddenly a loud banging rattled the door. We all jumped out of our skins. People usually just scratched and called, "Halloo!" I about broke the pots I was wiping, and wee Agnes started crying. She was only three and had no idea what the noise was. Mum had herbs and little tied bags scattered all over her lap, so I got up and went to the door.

As I opened the door, I could barely see from the feeble light outside, but it looked like three people. The man in front seemed like a giant. He was dark. His exposed face had piercing eyes, a long nose, and a deep frown. He had a long, dark riding cape over him. He wore trousers and riding boots like a Brit. Just behind him was the fat, pink-faced priest. His face glistened with sweat. Beside him I could see a woman. A shawl covered her head, and her face was too covered in darkness to see. I trembled where I stood. The last time I saw this priest was after my da died. It couldn't be good.

"Is Bridget MacTigue, the crofter, here?" The first man's voice boomed into our small living space, rattling the thin walls and causing my skin to prickle.

"Aye, I be here," Mum said, only a few short steps away.

She had managed to get the herbs off her lap and put a shawl over her head and shoulders. Agnes sniffed, clinging to her leg and holding a finger in her mouth. Her eyes were ringed with wet tears that slid down her cheeks and fell to the floor.

My mum was her normal calm exterior. She was always in control of herself. She showed no fear, but I could sense it. The air of the room became so thick that my bare arms prickled. I rubbed at them, but it didn't help.

The dark man took two giant steps, brushing me aside. I held onto the door so I wouldn't fall. The priest jumped to keep up. The woman slunk in with her head down. Her hands held a plain wooden cross in front of her chest. It was then that I saw that the priest was holding a large, shiny cross above his head. He waved it as he peered around our one-room cottage. We didn't have furniture to sit on nor food to share, as would normally be our custom.

"Please come in and be warm by our fire," my mum said, not a quaver in her voice.

I could not help my shaking, for a pall of doom seemed to seep into every corner of the room. It covered me like a chilling fog.

The big man pulled out a rolled-up tube. I knew it had to be paper, even though I had never seen it. He opened it with some difficulty since it was wound so tightly and wanted to stay that way. I could just make out small, black, scratch marks as he held it up to catch the firelight.

The light glowed behind it as he read, "Bridget MacTigue, by right and order of the Sacred Kirk of Mary the Redeemer, I, Sheriff of Moray, inform you that you have been accused of witchery."

I could tell he wasn't really reading. His voice was dull, and his eyes wandered. I doubted that any of the people in the room, except the pink-faced priest, could read. But his language was Latin. Maybe it was written in Latin, the language of the kirk.

"What do you say to the charge?" he bellowed.

"I am no' a witch!" exclaimed Mum loudly. Anger seeped onto her face. I could see her eyes narrow as she looked at the woman standing behind the priest. "Who has said so?" She picked up Agnes, who was crying again, and took a small step toward the covered woman.

The priest pushed his cross at Mum, almost hitting Agnes. Mum recoiled to protect the child. She put Agnes down and pushed her toward me. Agnes squealed and came running, hiding her face in my shift and encircling me in her arms.

I just held her there. Our fear mixed into terror as the priest shoved the cross at Mum again. *What does he want her to do?* She raised her hand and tried to grab it. I would have done the same.

"Name my accuser!" Mum yelled. "This be she, Janet MacTigue, my own kinswoman and cherished friend? Why, Janet? What wrong have I done you?"

With my mum's angry gaze upon her, Janet seemed to shrink. Her head sunk lower, and her shoulders caved in. She took a wincing step forward. The wooden cross held between her breasts was like a shield over her heart. She looked up at the priest, who was steadying his silver cross as if aiming a blade at my mum. She was only a little more than arm's distance away. If I had been she, I would have batted that hovering cross out of my way like a buzzing fly. But Mum stood waiting with her head up and her arms crossed. Janet wilted.

The sheriff looked down at her and demanded, "Janet, tell her how you lost your unborn child."

That gave her some courage. In a weak voice, she began her tale. "It was four days ago. I got out of the croft to look for eggs. We have hens, ya know."

"Yes, yes, go on," the big man said quickly, slicing the heavy air with his hand.

"When I returned to my door, I saw a wee bag hanging on it. This here be it." She held up a small bag, like the ones my mum made. Only I didn't recognize the material. "The very next day, the babe growing inside me was expelled. I have the bloody sheets to prove it." Her downcast eyes and turned face revealed the lie to me.

But I could see the men were convinced. "Liar," I said, unable to stop myself.

"Shut up, girl, or make it worse for yourself." The big man didn't even look at me.

"Why, Janet, I had no knowin' you were with child. And being a midwife, I usually know these things. You are a little old, aren't you?

Thirty-eight years, I think you have told me. That's old for carrying a pregnancy. That's old for getting pregnant, not that it doesn't happen, mind ya. Here, gentlemen are my herbal wares. And not a single one is put in a bag like that. Let me see it, Janet, and I'll tell you what's in it."

Mum reached out her hand. Janet recoiled, faking fear as far as I could tell. The priest stepped forward, holding his cross as if to beat back my mum. I wanted to run to her and let him hit me instead. But Agnes still sobbed around my legs, and I was held by the earth to that spot.

Mum threw up her arm to protect herself, and the cross came down on one of her thin wrists. We all heard the crunch of bones as her wrist broke from the blow. She screamed from the pain, and suddenly I saw the terror in her eyes.

"She is no' a witch!" I screamed, wanting to go to her so much that I suddenly grew strong and tall.

I picked up Agnes and fled to Mum's side. I looked at the tears in her eyes and felt defeat. I turned to face the priest, the evil, big man, and the even more evil woman, shielding my mum as she sobbed behind me.

"The priests will decide that, girl!" The big man tossed Agnes and me aside like a bag of wool with one hand and grabbed my mum around the waist. He hoisted her up under his arm where she hung, a dead deer ready for cleaning.

She managed to look at Janet and the priest, and between sobs, she said, "My children."

Janet had gotten control by now. Her story was being believed. She had a smirk on her face as they followed the big man out.

Agnes screamed, "Mum! Mum! Mummy!"

It was all I could do not to scream out too. My mum was not a witch. She wouldn't marry the devil if her life depended on it. But I didn't want to make things worse.

I left Agnes sitting in a pool of her own tears and ran after them. The big man had just mounted his horse and slung my mum face down in front of him; the carcass he was bringing home for dinner. I ran around to speak to her.

The woman and the priest had trouble getting on their horses, giving Mum time to whisper, "Take what food there is in the house and everything you can carry up to the cave! Do not stay in the house. Be quick, my love!"

With a jolt, the horse leaped away, galloping into the dark. I didn't think the big man knew I was there, and the priest and Janet were too preoccupied while trying to stay on their bolting nags to worry about me.

Then the night closed in. Darkness invaded my mind and my heart. As the tears dried from my eyes, I filled up with hate. With clenched fists and teeth, I followed the waning fire light back into the house where little Agnes lay on the dirt of the floor, trying to cry herself to sleep. I made her pallet for her, got her onto it, and got to work.

The cave was about a half hour away if I walked fast. It had been a favorite picnic spot in the laird's forest that no one seemed to know about. I wasn't allowed to go there by myself, but I often snuck away to play there, and I knew the route by heart, even in the dark.

I made three trips before Agnes woke up. I moved most of the food, blankets, and the few clothes we had. Too soon, the night was giving way to a gray morn, and I could hear Agnes crying and hungry in the empty croft. There wasn't much to eat. An old, wilted apple was about it. I had taken the oats, all the vegetables and anything green up to the cave. I cut up the apple and gave all the pieces but one to Agnes. I ate my piece and went out to a little three-sided shed beside the house. I figured some tools might be good to have. I knew there was an axe, and I almost cried when I thought I could use it as a weapon. I sure wanted to kill someone.

Then I heard Agnes scream. It was all I could do not to rush out to save her, but something stopped me. I looked between the slats of the shed wall. The scream stopped. I saw Agnes in a man's arms. He wore the clothes of a highland laird. His trews were belted with a wide leather belt, and he was gently handing over my sister to a woman. She was neat and clean with the airs of a lady, and Agnes stopped screaming and struggling.

Agnes pointed at the croft. "Thithter, tithter." Her lisp was so strong that the two couldn't understand.

Then a second man came out of the house. In his hand was an evil cross. "The witch didn't have much. What about the wee thing there? Any marks?"

"None," said the woman. "She's as normal as they come. She'll make an offering for the abbey and learn the Lord's ways. Don't you mind."

"At least one soul can be saved from the devil." The man touched his lips to his golden bronze cross. He flashed it around Agnes a bit.

She did the right thing, ooh-ing and ah-ing at it and trying to hold it. When he handed it to her, she actually brought it to her chest. I would have spit on it and thrown it in the dirt.

I couldn't be sure if that weren't the Laird MacTigue himself. It was only a feeling, but I was sure Agnes would be cared for, so I let her go. When Mum was freed, we would get her back. For now, my strength had left me, and I felt helpless to do anything. I slid to the floor of the shed and buried my face in my hands. No tears came.

The day was far into the morning when I finished gathering things I wanted to bring to the cave. I was just disappearing into the woods when movement on the road caught my eye. I moved in farther, but not too far to lose sight. I saw a group of crofters: Finley MacTigue; James and his brother, who we call Bull; and two others.

The men had axes and shovels and began to tear at our house. With a flint, they started a fire in the thatch hanging down from the roof. The men tore apart the shed and threw it on the house as it quickly turned into an inferno as hot as any hell. I could feel the heat even as far away as I was. This was what Mum was afraid of.

I watched as the house where I grew up turned to ashes, and what was left of my heart turned to char. The men were gone. No one was looking for me. They didn't care about me. They didn't know I existed. I was nothing.

In that moment, I felt alone and hollow. I hated those men, Janet, the fat priest, and the dark sheriff. I turned and trudged deeper and deeper into the woods, and the darkness that filled my mind was darker than any night.

2

THE CAVE

The cave wasn't that bad. The entrance was low, and a large blackberry bush hid it. Those were the worst berries to pick. Their claws were curved like a cat's, and even the backs of the leaves had them. I couldn't reach into a bush to get at its berries and come out without a scratch, but the danger was worth it because of their plump, juicy sweetness. They were my favorite.

Behind the bush, I saw a narrow strip of open ground where I could sidle by the thorns. It was like the bush didn't want to touch the rock for some reason. Nothing grew along the rock face. It was as smooth as polished copper. On the coldest days, I wouldn't want to touch it either. It would be as cold as ice.

Inside were two chambers. The front one was low. I stooped as I walked in. It was about ten paces long by six paces wide. I dropped my household things there. In the very back was a crack in the wall that was invisible if I didn't know to look for it. The front room had a dim light, but no light reached the back.

I moved through the crack into total blackness and dropped the blankets on the sandy floor. Back in the front room, I found the flint, a few dried leaves that had blown in, and a candle. I would have to get more candles. "One thing at a time," my da used to say.

I wadded up the leaves into a loose bundle and put them on the sand just inside the front door of the cave where a weak light filtered through. Striking the flint over and over with the striker produced a spark, but it took several attempts to get the leaf ball to catch fire. Once it did, I quickly lit the candle and dowsed the fire. I grabbed the food I brought from the house, and holding the candle in front of me, I went through the crack to the back of the cave.

It seemed like a fairy wonderland to me. It was a big room, like the hall at the kirk, and the flickering light revealed stone tables and chairs that were there one moment and gone the next as I moved the candle around. Nothing grew in the dark. The floor was clean, and nothing had been inside for a long time. I moved my few possessions into the backroom and brought in some dead leaves, twigs, and sticks to build a small fire for light. As the flames caught, I could see a hard stone floor above the sandy soft area where I was standing.

I slowly turned round and saw that a stream probably did flow through here sometimes. I was standing in the middle of it. It was too much to think about. I put the blankets down in the sand and watched the little fire as it crackled and burned.

The images of my own house burning came to me: my neighbors diligently working to put every last thing into the inferno, my mum's scream and the crunch of bones, and the evil that had invaded our home.

My life was gone. Tears came but soon dried. I couldn't cry. I couldn't feel. I was blank.

I woke up sometime late in the night. I went out to pee, and I could sense the moon on the going-down side of the horizon. I wanted to get an early start into town. My mum needed me, and I needed her. I tied a little bag around my neck. In it was the only money we had, two coppers.

It was pitch-black as I shimmied past the berry bush and began to move down the hill. That was when I noticed a light, right above my left shoulder. At first I ignored it. I was in a hurry, and I had to walk around trees and bushes. I didn't want to stop.

It's the moon, I told myself for a long time. But my curiosity finally stopped me, and I looked over my shoulder. There was nothing. I looked up and swiveled my head all around. I made a slow revolution where I stood. No light was coming from anywhere. Yet there was a dim glow, and I could see in the dark. My mind said it was the moon over my shoulder, but I didn't even see any stars. The treetops were thick, and the sky must have been cloudy.

I thought of the Good People, the ones who could use magic and lived in a different realm than ours. *Could they be helping me?* I'd heard the stories. Usually their help wasn't assistance at all. I was more surprised than scared though. I had too much to think about. Mysterious lights that made my dark wanderings easier were welcome. I wanted only one thing, to find my mum.

I was soon down at the road by the croft. The smell of smoke was thick. I stayed close to the hedge but decided not to cut across the plowed fields since the road would be faster. Keeping up a fast-moving pace, I made it unseen into the small village where I hoped my mum was still alive. It was early enough that the cocks hadn't started crowing yet.

It wasn't hard to find the gaol because it was the only stone building in the town, except for the kirk. Every other building was shuttered and dark, but the gaol's single window was wide open, and a bright light was falling out. I crept along the wall and crouched under the window. I could look in if I stood up on my toes. *Mayhaps Mum is in there in a cell.*

"Who woulda thought, poor Duncan's widow? Maybe she cursed him too?" a woman was saying.

"Nah," said a man as he leaned over the table and loudly slurped from a wooden bowl. "Taint no thing as a witch. Bitch maybe, but no witch. An' I think we know which one that Janet MacTigue is."

"You watch what ya says, Mr. Murphy!" the woman cried. "That silly priest and pompous sheriff are all worked up o'r this one now. There ha' always been somethin' funny about that Bridgett you mind, with her green growin' gardens and herbs. I say she deserves wot she gots."

"Maybe so, wife, but I am no' goin' ta say she murdered Janet MacTigue's unborn babe. No, let other people say so. No' I." He wiped the bottom of the bowl with a piece of rye bread and popped it in his mouth. "You be gettin' on 'ome now. Don' go disturbin' poor Bridget on yer way out. She'll be dead soon, and we don' need no curses throwed at us. Jus' leave 'er be."

The wife glared at him long and hard, as if that were exactly what she was planning to do. Then she let out a steamy breath of air, like a cat hissing at a dog, and grabbed some things off the table. With a straight back and raised head, she stomped the few steps to the door and looked back. The gaoler got up and opened the door for her, and she stomped out.

I slunk around the building, thinking to follow her. "Dead soon," the man had said. My mum was not dead yet. She could only be in one place, the pit where they left all of the condemned prisoners to starve and be humiliated before they were hung. It wasn't exactly in the road, but it was very near it. High Street it was called. The merchants built their houses there and sold their wares. The gaol was directly across from the pit, which was on the edge of an open verge where the hanging tree was also located. There were stocks for minor criminals and a chopping block for those who would lose their heads.

I watched Missus Gaoler from a safe distance, hoping she didn't see the light that stuck to me like a burr. It was still dark of the morn and more so due to the clouds. I did see some little item fall from her arms as she crossed the road, heading straight for the pit. She stood over the edge and peered down, but she didn't do anything. She soon toddled away. I crossed the road and was delighted to find the crust of peasant bread and a turnip the missus had dropped. My stomach growled, but I would save them for my mum.

I approached the pit with caution. *Could she really be in that stinking hole?* My beautiful mum's dark, almost black hair always fascinated me when I saw it flowing freely with its auburn traces around her face. I had her hair, but nothing else. I pushed my skinny girl body onto the ground. A thick metal grate covered the pit.

At first I thought no one was there. I could hear a faint trickle of water and feel the horrible cold and dampness rising with a smell of sickness from the hole. Ever so softly, I could hear what seemed like distant sobbing. My mum was down there somewhere, but I could not see.

"Mum? Mum?" I called softly through the grate. "Mum, it's me, Bernie."

The sobbing stopped. I could hear shuffling and a gasp.

"Bernadette?" I heard wonder in her voice. "What are you doing here? You shouldn't have come. But oh! How are you? Where is Agnes?

What has happened to you? Oh, my babes! My bairns!" She began to cry in earnest, deep, and wrenching sobs, the kind that wrack your whole body.

I began to cry too. "Mum! Mummy! What can we do?" I whined between the shaking sobs.

I was pitiful, hopeless, and alone. All I could do was cry. I laid my head and shoulder on the bars of the grate. I thought I could slide through the squares and take my mum in my arms, and she'd take me in hers. Somehow I had to get her out.

Very slowly we began to get control over ourselves as dawn was beginning to show itself. My mum was still covered up in the dark walls of the pit, but it's rough edges were beginning to show.

"Tell me, daughter. What has befallen you and your sister? Tell me quick."

"The croft is gone, burnt by our neighbors, the ones that work for the manse." I wiped my nose as it dripped and took a big sniff to stop the leak.

"That would be the Byron MacTigues then," she said. "What of your sister?"

"Before they burned our croft, it was looted. I was just coming back from loading the cave. Agnes had awakened earlier, and I gave her something to eat and made the last trip. Oh, Mum, I should have taken her with me, but she was content on her pallet, and I had my hands full." I was crying and rambling.

"It's not your fault, daughter. But, what next? Please tell me quick! Is she dead?"

"Non, no, no. I was in the shed when a well-to-do man and his wife came out of our house with Agnes. They said she had no mark and would make a good offering to the abbey. What does that mean, Mum?"

"It means that she had no mark of the devil and she will be well cared for as a sister in the church." I could tell she too was holding back tears, and when she shifted, she stifled a cry of pain. I could hear clanking. She was bound.

The light of the morning was shifting to dark gray, and a cock crowed, setting off others around the village. Soon High Street would become the busy village center that it was.

"Are you safe, Bernie?" Mum hissed.

I could just begin to make out her form huddled at the bottom of the rough pit.

"I'm in the cave with all the household things I could bring. I got everything I need for sure. Oh, I found this, a leaving from the gaoler's wife. Can you catch it?" I reached as far as I could through the grate, but even if she could stand up and reach, we couldn't touch. The piece of stale bread and small turnip were in my hand.

"Can you see where I am, child? Try to throw them at me. I'm fettered with heavy chains, and the sheriff was not kind to me before he left me with the gaoler."

I could now make out her gray form huddled among the walls, so I gently tossed, first the crust and then the turnip, but my eyes were filling with water again, and sight was lost to me.

"I have them, my love. I think you will be going now. It will be some days before they come for me. I want you to know the story from your mother's side. Come again of the morrow's dark, and I will tell the tale if I am able. Know that I'll not be coming home. You are old enough to make your life. But do not get caught here with me, or they are liable to put you in here too. I need you to hear my story, my love. Now go!"

Melissa J. Johnson

Her angry whisper was not about me. It was hopelessness that she raged against. As I slowly and carefully drifted into the bush around the forest verge, I took that hopelessness into me like fortifying food. It strengthened me with rage that began to sustain me as I walked back to my shelter and spent the following days of my life.

A TALE OF TWO WOMEN

With a small crackling fire, the cave was almost comfortable. I couldn't be bothered with the weather on the outside. All hell could freeze over, and I didn't care. I heard my da say that once. I couldn't remember why. *What if hell froze over?* I was pretty sure it would have no impact on the hell I was living in right here. *What could possibly be the difference between a hell down there and the hell right here?*

We never had much to do with religion in my house. Mum had taken me to the village kirk once in a while. The building impressed me with its huge columns, giant blocks of stone and colored glass in the windows. I liked to run my hand along the walls, where the gray stone was interspersed with bits of sharp black flint sunk into the mortar. It gave the kirk a patchwork look on the outside. We could never understand what the priests said. They didn't speak our language. On Sundays, they would sing and pray with little attention to peasants who might wander in to look around and maybe leave feeling blessed. I never felt blessed.

My da said his kirk was the forest. When he said that, he always followed it with, "But don't tell anyone." That was because, if Mum heard him say it, she would hiss, "Duncan MacTigue!" That was when he would go outside, giving me a wink as he walked through the door. The fat priest said he was irreverent.

As I sat next to the fire, I figured out what irreverent was. I hated that fat priest and his kirk. My eyes were stinging with anger. I really needed to hurt something. But there was no one to hurt and nothing to use but a sharp knife. I got it out of the pile from the house and sat back down. It was in a leather sheath.

Mum was very careful to take care of important things. This knife was the only one we had, and not only did it cut vegetables for meals, it butchered whatever small game we caught. Once we even had a pig. Mum kept it sharp, and I watched her do it.

I slid the small blade out of its sheath. It could be used to kill. A dagger it was—long, lean, and murderous by my own reckoning. I began by cutting off my hair. From the top of my ear, I grabbed hanks of long and tangled black hair. With one slice, the hair would come away, and I threw it into the fire. Once my mum had looked at me so kindly and proud and told me my hair was my crowning glory. Right now, it was a weight around my head. It was a mark of identification.

"Bernadette," it declared.

I was no longer that girl. I was someone else, a terrible person. I cut and whacked at my hair until its acrid smell filled the cave and I could hardly breathe. My smell, the odor of burnt hair, Bernie, was burning. Now my name was Bern.

I found a needle and coarse thread and made a slice down the bag I used to carry stuff in. I opened the seam at the bottom and made myself a pair of britches. The rope at the top of the sack became the belt that held them around my wee, thin waist. I cut a swath around my coarse woolen shift to shorten it and used pieces of that for two pockets. To stop the wool from fraying, I turned a section of it up all around and sewed it with small stitches. I could pass for a boy for awhile, maybe for a long time, long enough to hide. I could blend in better than a girl could. Perhaps I could even become strong and get my mum out or find revenge.

I stepped outside for the first time as a boy. The world was gray, and water dripped from the trees, making a plopping sound as it hit the moist ground cover. Each drip was a tear I refused to shed. The whole forest cried for me. Only the ravens laughed.

I was squatting for a pee when one large blue-black bird landed on a tree branch in front of me. It looked down, craning its head and tipping one black eye at me for a better view. I stared up at it, daring it to come down and fight. I clenched my fists tight.

"What!" it suddenly said. It straightened up and stamped its feet.

I was done with my business but stayed there.

"What!" it said louder. It snapped its wings and pointed its huge, sharp beak at me. "What, what, what!" With each sound, its eyes seemed to do sparkling pinwheels in its head.

It wasn't asking a question. It was making a demand. Its mate landed in another tree, and she began snapping her wings and demanding, "What! What! What!"

I made a fast retreat into the cave. Both birds seemed to be demanding something of me. I could hear them from inside the cave for a long while. Ravens were scary birds. Some grannies thought ravens were messengers, delivering communication from the dead to the living. Maybe it was the Good People keeping an eye on me. Or perhaps it was just a couple of ravens. I was too angry and tired to worry about it. I would fight those who might try to get in my way, be they human or magical beings.

I didn't even remember going to my pallet, but I found myself rolled up in a blanket in the darkness of my cave with just a few glowing embers in the fire, tiny promises of light gleaming out at me. The orb of light over my left shoulder was what I could see by. It always seemed to be there in the dark, but I did not always notice it. I found the blade and took a couple of practice stabs in the air. I tied it with extra strips from my shift to my right leg. My new britches would cover it up. Never mind that I hadn't ever used a blade before. I knew I could if I needed to, and I would if the urge arose. I walked out feeling powerful and mean. *Let nothing stand in my way.*

The feeling went completely away an hour later as I approached the pit from the forest. I had forgotten to eat, and my stomach was so empty that I could swear it was eating me. I suddenly realized that I didn't want my poor mum to see my mutilated head.

I leaned over the grate anyway and whispered, "Mum?"

I heard the soft rattle of chains as she shifted. "Daughter, just in time." Her voice was soft and weak.

My heart leaped into my throat, and rough tears seeped out of my eyes. I didn't think I had any water left in them.

"My good girl, you have always been my delight." Her thin voice quavered ever so slightly.

"Mum," I began.

"No, don't speak, Bernie. Just listen. I have much to tell you. Some of this is not for a child's ears, but I think you have turned into a woman overnight. I need you to know the truth—for good or for bad. Who knows what the fates have in store for you, my daughter? My fate has been sealed by a jealous and evil friend. What did I have to make her so jealous? That question has been plaguing me since I first saw it in her face that night. It seems like an age now. I feel I've been in this pit forever, and my death will be a relief. Sometimes that happens."

I wanted to jump up and scream into the dark, "No! This does not happen to good and loving people!" But I stayed still. Only water drained from my eyes like small, silent creeks.

She continued, "My anguish turns to you and what your life will be. I want to counsel you, and yet I don't have the words. 'Try to find your own happiness is all I can think of to say.'"

I wept silently. I slumped over the grate and put my arm under my eyes so the wool sleeve could stem the flow. This only caused me to gasp and sniffle, but it could not be helped. I took great choking sobs that only scared me more. Someone might hear and come with piles of garbage to throw down on her.

"Hush, my Bernie, this is hard enough for me." Her voice quavered. She was holding back. I knew I could do it too. "We don't have much time left, so listen and be still." There was a pause. "I first met my accuser, Janet, before your father died and before Agnes was born. She was a friend of a customer who introduced us one day when we met on High Street.

"When Agnes was born, Janet became a true friend. She came by the house often and brought food that she could spare. Sometimes she watched the bairn so I could go pick nettles or other herbs in the forest. We shared the bounty out of our gardens, gossip about town, laughter, and sadness. When yer da died, she helped around the house. Our friendship deepened for these simple reasons.

"Janet's husband is an accountant for the wool merchant in Forresgem, so her means were much greater than ours. There were moments, I have to admit, when I wondered why she chose to befriend me. But maybe since her kids were grown and out of the house, she had time on her hands and needed diversion. I didn't think about it too much.

"You remember, she had two boys. They were already fifteen and sixteen, and I think. King James had pressed both of them into service at that time. They were just foot soldiers. You know, fodder for the king, as we say," she paused.

"I never realized that Janet was so full of hate. She must have been seething inside for her to do this deed," Mum suddenly said.

Seething was not a word I used, but just then, I knew that I too was seething. I understood the hate that Janet must have felt because I too hated.

"Your da and I dreamed of better for you. I could see you with your long, beautiful hair attracting some man from the manse and you becoming the lady of a croft beside the laird's. Maybe even working for the laird somehow; in the gardens or kitchen. Or, perhaps some son of a merchant on High Street taking you as his wife. You are smart and a quick learner. I think you could be good at letters and perhaps become a scribe or teacher. It's not unheard of. You are way above the intelligence of most children your age, which is why I know that you will be fine after I am gone."

I wanted to scream, "No, no, no! I can't live without my mum! What devil in all his evil has created this realm?" But I stayed as quiet as I could. Convulsive shivering wracked my exhausted body.

I took huge gulping breaths and grabbed the iron grate with tight fists. My brain screamed, *this is not right!* I gritted my teeth tight and squeezed my eyes shut. If I could have gnawed on the metal and freed my mum, I would have started chewing.

Mum continued, "After your da died, I gradually learned how to live without him. I felt no need to take a man to bed. Don't be shocked, love. You know what I'm talking about."

I knew. It was hard to live in a one-room croft without some idea of what your parents were up to in the night. It was never talked about, and I didn't really know the details. I wasn't even sure if it were pleasure or pain, except that mum and da never made a fuss and always seemed content. I knew they loved each other. It must have been pleasure.

"One day, Janet was visiting. She brought some mending, and I had some stitching to do. So we sat and talked. She told me that she had joined an unusual group of women. That got my attention. She said one of the priests was up from St. Andrews, and he had this strange idea to teach women about the Bible. You know the Bible is in Latin, and women, even most men, don't read or speak Latin. This makes going to service at the church useless for the most part. I always thought I would like to know what the priests know. They seem so understanding of God's demands. It intrigued me to think that, even though we couldn't read or understand Latin, we might be able to learn God's will from a priest."

The deep dark of night gave way almost without our knowing. Little details of the rough pit walls began to show through, and my poor mum's dark figure was becoming clear to my eyes.

"Oh, my big girl, I fear it is growing light out and time for you to run. The story will have to be finished on the morrow. Finish I will because I know they are making haste to bury me. Run and hide, my daughter. Be careful, and come back to me in the dark."

She could not hide her sobbing now. It was clear and anguished. I could not speak, and I could not see for the water filling my eyes, but I obeyed and stumbled off behind a thick bush in the forested verge. I needed to sit there to wipe my flowing eyes and nose before I walked away.

I wasn't sure where I was going. I felt like a wraith. I had no skin or bones. Pieces of me were floating in the air. There was nothing to hold me together, and the slightest move or breath of air would cause me to fall apart. I sat for a long time. My mind stopped, and I was still.

Just before the gray dawn broke, a man came walking down the High Street. I thought he might be a merchant on some early business in the village. But he was looking from side to side as if he weren't quite comfortable being where he was or maybe even being who he was.

He stopped at the pit and kneeled down on both knees as if he were getting ready to pray. Then after a quick look around, he got on all fours, and he was talking to my mum. Or she was talking to him. I couldn't hear a word. After a couple of still minutes, broken only by his fervent glancing around, he pulled a small cloth bag out of his pocket and lowered his arm into the pit to drop the bag for my mum.

Food? A friend, I thought, *but a very curious friend.*

After dropping the small bag and looking around, he got up and walked briskly in the same direction he'd been going. I decided to follow him.

He turned down the first narrow trail that he came to; walking between the wool merchant's house and the fabric maker's. It looked like the wool merchant was preparing to build a new stone house over his wooden one. I saw large piles of stones around the place, and already a couple of men worked there. The thick hedge soon came up and hid them from my view. The trail was straight and short. It came out on the road up from High Street, and my quarry was now heading toward the kirk.

I could see lights behind shuttered windows. The buildings in this part of the village were not so grand as the ones on High Street. They were more than just hovels. These were foremen working for merchants, a lawyer or two, and people in industry. The man moved quickly up the road.

My bare feet stepped up the pace until I was running. If he turned, he would see me, but I was just a small boy. He would take no notice. A donkey brayed, which started a whole series of sounds, from a horse's whinny to dogs and chickens. Even some geese got in on the noise. The village was waking up as the man entered the kirk through a side door.

There were no windows I could use to look into the church. It reminded me of a huge ship, maybe three huge vessels. I saw one once when Da took me down to the dock at Firthlanding. It was being loaded with bags of wool, and the men and bags were so tiny next to the hulk of the vessel. Even though our kirk was small compared to the manse of the laird, it loomed above me.

The door the man went in was locked. I had to go in the front. It was quiet and cold inside, a kind of solid cold that permeated everything. The columns of the empty space made me feel like I was enclosed in a block of ice, like the ones they cut out of the lake in the winter.

The quiet saturated everything. It felt wrong to be here. The stones and the painted glass stared down, accusing anyone who entered. I wasn't sure what I'd done, but I was certain it was something. There were statues in white, stone coffins elaborately carved with fierce animals, and fiercer men. A huge gold-painted cross, with the dying body of their god in his torture, dominated the end of the hall in front of a single row of benches. His eyes were open, blood from a crown of thorns dripped down his face, and I could not evade his glare.

He accused me. I felt like cowering behind the bench. That was where the laird's family sat when they came to the kirk. Perhaps it was for them to feel the accusing look of that tortured man. The common people stood around near the entrance. For us, this god was far away and out of touch.

Suddenly my anger came back. *What did I do to deserve this god's accusations?* I climbed over the wooden bench and plunked myself down with a force that caused the bench to rattle. I glared at the god hanging there.

"What did I ever do to you?" I said in a low voice that surprised me. It was almost a growl. "What?"

"This is ridiculous!" a man yelled from behind a door in the corner of the kirk hall. "I want this to stop now!" It was muffled but clear enough. It jolted me out of my anger.

Another voice calmly replied, "It's too far gone now, Dougal. We must let the process continue. There is no turning back."

It was the pink-faced priest. I knew it. I moved quietly to the door and had my ear to the crack so things were a wee bit clearer. I'd wager the other man was the one that had visited my mum.

"Bridget MacTigue is not a witch!" the first man yelled.

"Ah, but she is. Her own friend, Janet, has accused her, and our good sheriff, Robert, has tested her. What more proof do ye need, Dougal?"

"Our good sheriff Robert tested her all right! He used her body in the most vicious way for his own sordid pleasure. And then he put her in the pit where, if she doesn't die from exposure, he will kill her. No doubt to hide his own corruption. Why in God's name did Janet do this? That is what I don't understand."

I couldn't prove it, but it sounded like Dougal was crying.

"Well, I'm sure, if Janet had a reason, it was for self-preservation. Remember, James also accused Bridget," said the fat priest.

"Please, Brother Peck, you know that, at times like these, people just want to blame someone for their failures. If you pressed James, I'm sure the truth would be that he couldn't perform abed with his wife due to his guilt for being with a whore. There are many reasons for flaccidness."

"What about Drew MacEwen's stallion at stud? A horse doesn't have flaccidity issues, but his did. No, I am sorry Dougal, but there are too many strange occurrences lately to pass them by. It's the work of common witchery for sure. Where are you going? Don't you have a lesson to teach?"

"I've cancelled. I'm going to pray for our souls."

I heard an inner door slam and, much more softly, another slam as Dougal made his way into the depths of the kirk. There was a swoosh-swoosh sound of the heavy priest's sandals on the cold stone floor. He was coming my way. I bolted down the kirk hall as fast as I could and out the front door, where I assumed a casual pose and walked down the steps to High Street.

I was anything but calm. I shook to my core. The man was trying to save my mum. *What should I do?* I needed to return to the cave and think, but it was late morning, and I still hadn't eaten. I was needing food. I asked myself, *Should I beg or spend the pence in my bag? And if I were going to beg, where would I go?*

There weren't a lot of beggars in Forresgem, at least not when I'd been there. I walked up High Street, just wanting to get away. I wasn't starving yet, but it wouldn't be long. I could feel the heat of the sun on my sheared head, but the chill that had sunk into my bones was permanent. I could hear the clanging of the smithy, doves voiced their annoying crying calls in the trees at the edges of the road, and the day seemed normal in the village.

My bare feet avoided the rocks almost without my knowing, and food smells came to me as I passed by open doors. None of it was real. My body needed food, but even that could not overcome the frost covering my heart. I turned into the only eatery in town.

It didn't have a boarded floor, just dirt, and a lad about as old as me was slowly sweeping it with a very limp broom, picking up the big chunks of spilled food, stones, or things people dropped. At the last minute, I decided to pretend I couldn't talk. I boldly walked up to him as any boy would and pointed to my open mouth.

"Eh there! Wot? Cat's got ye tongue?" He paused in his slow sweeping to look into my mouth.

I shook my head no and held out both hands, palms up. I then pointed to my mouth again with my eyebrows raised. It seemed like a universal symbol to me.

"Oh, yuz wantin' food. Ave ya no coin?"

Yes and no, I nodded.

"Milly!" he yelled. "We gots a laddie here a beggin'. Want me ta shows 'im the door?"

"Eh now, watcha hollerin' about?" Milly was a large, round woman with flushed red, scratchy cheeks, a none too stylish gray cap over her hair, and an apron over her shift that had seen better days. The folds over her eyes were so large as to make her eyes look shut, but she popped them out briefly to take a look at me.

"Beggar boy, are ye? Go out back. You can check the slop bucket afore I give it to the piggies. Hurry on out. Be gone afore midday meal." She pointed to the back where I could see the kitchen, and there was a door to the yard.

The slop bucket was right outside the door. It was a banquet at the laird's manse to my mind. I grabbed some gristle-covered chicken legs; a long hank of bubbly fat, probably beef; a large floret of broccoli with a little mold on it; and a rock-hard crust of brown wheat bread. It was a splendid meal. A small piece of moldy cheese was the last treasure I fished out of that bucket. I only had to fight the huge black flies that were buzzing around, and it was all free. I stuffed my pockets and left through the yard.

As I walked back to the cave, I chewed on the gristle end of a bone, cracking it and sucking out the marrow. I threw it down behind me, no longer caring if people saw me. No one would pay any attention to me. I was careful when I got back to the forest though, not to be seen using my trail to the cave.

Before I went in, I walked over to the nearby stream. I lay down with my face to the rushing water and took a long, cool draught. After rinsing my oily hands, I went into the cave and slept.

I dreamed that a huge raven walked in through the crack in the cave. He stood over me, cocking his head to get a better look at my sleeping body. I knew he was there, but I couldn't move. I couldn't call out, and I was stiff as a board. The bird plunged his black beak into my chest. It closed around my heart, and with a jerk of his head, he pulled it out of my body and gulped it down. Just as quickly, his own heart leaped out of his body and entered the hole where my own heart had been. I flailed my arms out, but I didn't have time to find my voice.

The bird took two hopping jumps toward the opening and fled out the cave. My eyes flung open, and I took a huge gasping breath. My heart was beating so hard that I thought for an instant it might fall out the hole in my chest. I covered it with my hand, but there was no gaping wound. I sat up. The cave was completely dark. Not even an ember glowed from the fire. I could feel no hole. Nothing was damaged. My shirt was not even torn.

It took me sometime to calm down, and I knew it was time to go to the pit when I noticed my light shining dimly. I ate a couple bites of wrinkled onion and finished off the small piece of moldy cheese. Then I headed out to rescue my mum.

4

THE TALE CONTINUES

I ran the whole way into the village. Darkness covered everything, but my light never failed. The air was so wet with leftover rain that I was dripping by the time I made it to the edge of the pit, cold and dripping. I should have brought a blanket. I could have left it for my mum.

I splashed down onto the grate.

"Daughter, is that you?" Her voice was cracked, and her breath gurgled. Chains rattled softly.

"Aye, tis, Mum."

She began coughing in huge bouts of wet, hacking bursts. Even though my heart was already broken and removed from my chest, the tears were back again.

"Mum, yer sick. Let me fetch you some herbs to help with that cough," I pleaded.

"Shush, child. Don't leave me now. You must hear my tale. Now, stay silent, and I will finish my story.

"I went to that Bible meeting with Janet. It was held in the monk's dining hall where there was a table and some benches. Four other women were there. You don't need their names. They are blameless and innocent. Janet introduced me to the teacher, whose name is Father Dougal."

Now I knew the priest that I followed into the church. I needed to get his help. It wasn't too late to free my mum, but I couldn't do it without him.

"Did you ever hear that there are nine total hells, Bernadette? Each one is for a different kind of sinner. This comes from a book that is popular just now, even though a man from Italia wrote it one hundred years ago. His name was Dantie or Dante. He called his book *Comedia*, which you might know means funny. It is really not very funny. Hell is not funny."

"Dougal and Janet seemed to have a special friendship from the beginning. I noticed that he spoke a little less forward to her. Do you know what I mean? Your da did it to me when he wanted something. It's like a softer kind of man voice."

I wasn't sure what she meant, but I kept my mouth shut.

"I think the others noticed it too. They couldn't help but notice that Dougal usually talked to Janet. He looked at her when he was teaching, listened to what she said, and even allowed her to argue with him. That was the most shocking. After going to several classes, I began to feel like I was watching an old married couple bickering about this or that.

"She was always looking her best too. Nothing wrong with that, of course. I hope that you will also always look your best, my darling, even after you wed. It just helps. People will treat you better."

Looking my best was the last thing I cared about right then. No beggar boy, nor beggar girl, had a choice of fine clothing.

"In this case, her best was done-up hair and fancy, stylish hats. I think Janet was too concerned with hats. Of course, women are supposed to cover their heads and bind their hair, but Janet figured out how to cover her head and hair and still flaunt it. She does have beautiful golden locks. Why be so dressy in front of a monk? These monks take vows of celibacy. Oh, dear Bernie, do you know what that means?" she exclaimed, followed by a series of wracking coughs.

"Do you have water, Mum?" I cried when I could stand it no more.

"Yes," she whispered between coughs. She quieted.

"No, Mum, I don't know what it is," I said softly.

I could hear her swallowing. She cleared her throat gently. "That means monks and priests vow never to get married." Then as a second thought, she said, "They cannot have relations with women, the kind that make babes. They are married to the kirk. No women allowed."

"I understand," I said.

Really I didn't. *Married to the kirk? What is that all about? If priests can marry a thing that's not a woman, what else can they do? And why do they not want women?* I was young, but even I knew of the attraction between men and women, girls and boys. Mum had spoken of it, and my da teased me sometimes. Boys were better players than girls were. They thought up monsters, wild animals, and war play with sticks and rocks, and they ran and climbed trees. I preferred boys to girls as friends. I'd rather be married to one than to a large, cold building. I knew what had to happen for babes to be born, but seeing the act in chickens, dogs, or pigs sure didn't make me want to try it.

"For a time, I thought Janet was showing off her wealth. But as time went by, the attention and the looks told me something else. I began to wonder if there were a special feeling the two had for each other. I thought maybe they were in love, like me and your da were once."

"I see." I suddenly got it ... or part of it.

"This is where the tellin' gets a little hard, so please don't judge me, daughter. I will tell you true." There was a long pause. "Dougal was a comely man that was well built under his priest's garment. I believe he was showing his best self for Janet, as she did for him.

"After some time of our weekly class, Janet was going to be gone for a time. Usually when she was gone, Dougal cancelled the class, so we weren't surprised when he did it again. But that Sunday when I was peddling my wares in the kirk, I was shocked when he stepped up to me and asked if I might want to keep our usual afternoon class time to go over some of our more difficult studies. I said I would like that. I didn't have anythin' planned, so why not? I had no knowin' that he had not invited the others too.

"I have to admit to you, my daughter, and this is something you may not want to hear, but I was attracted to this man. He knew so much! When I looked into his eyes, I could feel doors opening into other places and other people. My small life seemed so minor. I was nothing in the face of his knowledge, and I wanted more. I knew nothing would ever come of our relationship as teacher and student, as priest and woman.

"I went to the kirk dining room as usual the next day. He had not invited the other women. I was the only one. He seemed suddenly to be quite shy, not looking at me and stumbling over his words, but as we finished with the greetings, we got into our studies. He decided to talk about the second of the nine circles of hell.

"I will confess that I am not a good Christian woman in some regards. I never could understand the excessive interest that the kirk has with hell. How could it possibly be any worse than what we do to each other right here? The old beliefs are still available through our grannies, and this is how I was raised. We had our holy people who kept our rituals and helped us when we needed it. That is how my mum learned about herbs and healin'. So this study of the hell realms was new to me."

I knew I was having a direct experience of hell. Hell was my daily companion. What else could it be?

"Sins of incontinence, he called it. These are the people who have trouble controlling their desires. That's like someone always wanting more than his share. You know what desires are? Like wanting more food after we've finished what we've got. Or seeing something at the market like a beautiful bolt of fabric that you just have to have but can't. You come home and dream about what you will do with it, like sew it into a gown and look so lovely, like a regular lady. Or a friend has a new necklace, and it is so lovely that all you can think about is havin' it fer yer own."

I guessed I had never experienced desire like that. At least not that I could recall at that moment. Those weren't things I craved. Maybe it was a grown-up feeling.

"This sin includes lust, which is the way a man and woman can feel about each other when they want to make a baby. Can you understand, my love?" Her voice was a low gurgling growl.

"Yes, Mum," I told her, but really I did not. "Do you mean love, Mum?" I had heard bards sing of love on market day, but I had never felt that kind of love.

"It is a kind of love, daughter. Only it is too much. Does that make sense? No? Let me try again. It is okay for married couples to have lust, for them it is called love. But for people who are not married, in the minds of priests who are married to the church, that activity is lust. And lust is forbidden. It is a sin to love someone you are not married to."

"I understand," I whispered.

My mother stopped for a moment. She cleared her throat with a raspy cough. "In this level of hell, those who died with the sin of lust are cursed to wander in battering winds, tornadoes throwing up splinters of icy rain, and small, cutting stones. This is the condition they are in forever and ever.

"At the end of this lesson, the priest put his hand over my hand on the table. I almost recoiled. Only because he was a priest did I remain alone with him. We were in the kirk dining room, which Father Peck often visited. I was not concerned. His hand was very gentle, and he was looking so fiercely into my eyes that I just thought pious righteousness had overcome him. I was a chaste woman. Your da was the only man I had ever been with. The priest was an attractive man, as I have said, but his being a priest was enough for me."

An overwhelming silence came from the pit. "Mum?" I whispered.

"He asked me to come back sooner so we could review all the hells before Janet got back. She would not want to go over them again, he said. I laughed and agreed. He showed me out the kitchen door, and I felt him standing a wee bit close, almost touching.

"When we met two days later, we talked about the third hell for gluttons. Those are people who take too much. In a room full of people, they don't see anyone else. Their punishment is to lie in vile slush, which their own excrement produces. A constant, foul, and icy rain falls on them. When he talked about greed, he reached over the table and brushed my lips with his fingertips. The whole time he had been talking, he had me transfixed. I looked into his eyes and he into mine, and slowly my body was awakening to the presence of him. I couldn't help myself. I knew, if we continued to meet alone, I would be in love with him. Do you know what I mean, Bernie? It is important that you understand."

"Yes, Mum," I said. "I don't know what you mean about your body.

I suppose these things are between a man and a woman, and I am too young to know."

"My smart girl that is the truth of it. I am taking away your innocence. For that, I am sorry. But I must go on. You must know the truth. It was lust. I was perplexed and confused. Why would this man have any interest in myself at all? Was he playing with Janet this way too? Or could he possibly have an interest, maybe even love, for me? I was falling in love with him. Or maybe it was my body that was falling. I marveled at the changes it was going through.

"I won't go into the details, but being an older woman, many of my body's ways had been shut down. I didn't need a man. I was done having babes. I was content as I could be after the loss of my husband. Suddenly I was enlivened. My body was responding as if its youth had been returned. You'll know what I mean someday.

"By the eighth lesson, he was holding me with his eyes. I stood up to go, and as I reached for the door, his soft, warm hand held my arm and turned me to face him. He embraced me and I he. He kissed my covered head and my neck and held me so close that I could feel his heart beat, and for a moment, I couldn't tell where his body ended and mine began. It was a pure blending of body and soul."

I had to hold in a gasp. Even I knew that men and women did not touch each other under any circumstances. I didn't know about sin, but this was not proper. *How could my own mum allow this to happen?*

"It was you who was bewitched!" I yelled. And as soon as I did, I was sorry.

She began a cough so ragged that I believed it might stop her heart right there. In between coughs, she mumbled, "No, no, no." When she could, she began again. "It seems like that to your young mind, but someday you'll know what love is between a man and woman. I wish I would be there to help you and show you the way, but for now, just know that love is the sweetest of emotions. Your da and I had as fine a love as anyone could want. This priest and I had a love, or so I thought. Even as I went out the door with his sweet kiss on my neck, I was thinking how this would be over as soon as Janet returned. How could we continue this way anyway? My mind just couldn't see it. But my body wanted it.

"Janet did return, of course. Class went back to usual. My private lessons stopped. The priest wasn't quite the same though. He seemed a little confused as to how to continue the lessons. He looked at Janet, but he shared looks with me that must have been obvious to her. Of course, she blamed me, and she was perfectly right. I don't know what I had done to deserve the priest's attention. He did say once that he was lonely. He thought I must be lonely too. I wasn't. I was perfectly content, just my girls and me. But I succumbed to his attention. Some kind of sin on my part, I guess. I wanted him, I believed him, and that was my mistake.

"Janet turned against me and cut me with her words at any opportunity. It served me right. What was I thinking to get so involved with a priest? And here I am, on a whim of Janet's. The only way she could figure how to get rid of me and punish me at the same time. I am lost for the jealousy of a friend."

I was stunned to silence. I had no understanding of the ways of women and men. I could feel the wrongness and a growing hate for the woman who would destroy my mum.

"Bernie, my love, are you still there? I 'ave not wounded you so deeply you cannot forgive? It is late now. I fear the sun rises, and you must flee if you haven't yet."

"I'm here, Mum." I sniffed. I didn't even know I was crying. "I can't lose you." I sobbed. "What do I know? I have nothing without you."

"Your future is now yours to make, dearest. I give this telling to you as a lesson. Choose yer friends wisely. Be careful of men who want to love you. Love yourself enough to make the right decisions. I have nothing more to give you. I'll help if I can from wherever my death puts me. I'm pretty sure it won't be hell as described by this Dantie, who said he'd been there and lived to write about it. No, my God is not as cruel as that. He watches out for growing lassies, he does.

"Now go. Don't come back. I won't be here tomorrow or anywhere. Do your best, my own sweet bairn. Look forward and love yourself. Know you are loved! Go!" She shouted, falling into an angry cough that stopped my heart and caused me to leap up off the grate.

"Go …" she whispered.

As I turned away, she added, "Love."

5

MEETING DOUGAL

I snuck away like a whipped puppy. My own life, what was left of Bernadette, seeped through my feet into the earth with every step. My Self left my body for good. A shell of a twelve-year-old wandered out onto High Street in the opening hours of the day. I was the only movement. Not a wisp of air floated by me. Not a flash of light from a lantern or warming fire showed through the watery haze of my eyes. The earth took my Self without complaint until I was an empty husk. I might as well be dead.

Without knowing it, my body made its way to the bench in the kirk. As I stared up at the agonized statue of the helpless God, I could not understand how these people could choose such a weak man as their hero. *How could he have gotten into this predicament, and why was he blaming me for it?* It was the look in his eyes. I felt his blame and my helplessness.

"What could I do? I can't live without you." A woman's pitiful voice came from behind the door.

"Poor, poor woman." It was Dougal. "What you have done ... What you have done is murder! Do ya not see it? And fer what? For yer own imaginary need. A need that yer own man must fulfill. Not a priest. Don't ya see?"

I moved without a sound to stand motionless by the thick door. I could feel no solidity. I felt that my body could disappear, blending into the coarse wood of the door, and that I would stay there trapped in the wood. But I didn't. I was numb. The cool, rough surface of the door was a relief, something solid I could feel with my skin.

"Woman, you need to confess and do it now," he said, raising his voice to an angry pitch.

"But, Father." I could hear a chair or table scrape on the floor. "I have just made my confession to you."

"You need to go to the sheriff and tell him the truth of your lies. That will be the only way to undo this grave sin of yours. Don't touch me, woman. You have forgotten yourself." His voice was sharp. I could sense it cutting through her like a blade.

"You wound me, Dougal." I imagined her straightening. "I cannot go to Sheriff Robert now and tell him that Bridget is not a witch." Her voice was no longer whining. "Who is to say that she is not?"

"Janet, God will see you as the only spell caster here if you do na' make it right."

"I will repent." Tears were in her voice now. "I will. But I will do it in the kirk, and I will do it with your arms around me!"

"Janet! Do you not hear yourself?" His voice had reached a high pitch. If I were him, I would be wanting to hit something.

"It's your doing, Dougal, priest, father, monk," she said, growling. "You turned my mind with your soft eyes boring into my heart. With your calm conversation, your attention, and kind words lovingly said. You are not pure, Father Dougal!"

She threw those words in his face, and I felt him flinching with each one. I imagined him covering his face in his hands, as Janet's open, threatening body stood menacingly in front of him, close enough to smell and to touch. I felt for the blade under the wool of my breeks. My hand shook. He would stop me. I knew. I was too small.

"That is why I am leaving," he said.

"No!" A chair scraped the floor.

"Let go of me, woman!" the priest yelled. "Sit and get a hold of yerself. I have already notified Father Peck, and I will be going into seclusion. You have misinterpreted me, and so, yes, I have sinned and failed. I am not pure, non. I am a man. That is all. Now, goodbye."

Janet shrieked, and with a bustle of skirts, she ran for the door to the outside, the same door he had walked in the day before.

Even if Janet did confess, nothing would change. She would be of no help. I knew what the sheriff had done to me mum. I knew that men often hurt women, especially important men who felt that women were theirs for the taking. That the sheriff was cruel, I had no doubts. Janet would not be able to convince him to let my mum go.

Just as I was turning from the door, where I stood listening, it opened. I wasn't fast enough to get away, and I didn't care.

I turned to face the door, and there was Dougal with his pinched face and red-rimmed eyes staring at me. He quickly realized that I had been listening at the door.

"It's okay," he said under his breath. His shoulders drooped, and his head lowered. "A mere lost boy. Can I help you, son? We haven't much food but a little bread from the laird's kitchen. Some lard to put on top..."

"Naw," I managed to say and turned to go sit on the bench. I wanted him to leave me, but I realized he was the last hope to save my mum.

He came and sat by me. He clasped his hands together, bending over with his elbows on his legs as if he were praying. "Shall we kneel and pray?"

"Non." I wasn't about to pray to this tormented god. I needed a strong god who would ride in on a thunderbolt and lop off heads and then pick my mum out of the pit, heal her, and put the both of us somewhere safe and happy. This god was not capable.

"Oh," said Dougal, "do not turn away from God in your time of need, my young son. I hear the anguish in your no. Tell me your troubles. I think you will find I can understand. Not being a perfect priest, I am a perfect man with all the faults and blemishes that go with that."

"Why did you torment my mother?" I asked.

He looked at me long and hard.

"Aye, Bridget is my mum." I looked deeply into his eyes, just wanting to see something strong in him. I did not see it.

"Oh my God!" He looked up to the heavens. "Not this. I am killt and killt again. I can never escape the tragedy of my dearest Bridgette. I am undone. I have forsaken my loving God and destroyed a family, mayhaps two. The one unknowing through my love as a priest. The other knowing through my passion as a man."

"A priest cannot be a man. Maybe that is the problem with this religion you profess." I stood up to go. I could not see anything useful coming from talking to this weak priest. I knew he was worthless to aid my mum.

"I loved yer mum," he said to the floor. "For her, I would have quit my calling."

"Then go save her. She loves you." These last words hurt to say, but I knew it was the truth.

He shook as he wept silently. Huge drops of water struck the floor and seeped between the cracks. Down into the earth they soaked. The earth must take all of our misery. His shoulders heaved with his sobs, and I walked through the kirk and out onto High Street, where the morning was well begun, but the sky was dark and ominous. My feet and legs seemed unattached, and my back was hunched like an old granny. Hopelessness settled on me like a heavy burden.

6

THE WITCH'S RIDE

My old body was heavy and weak. My limbs did their own bidding. I remembered when once I was young and active, without a care. Now I was in pain, a deep hurt that seemed not to be of my body but of my own deepest self. My senses seemed to be leaving me. My eyes couldn't see clearly. My normally scratchy, woolen clothes hung on me, but I felt naked. I didn't care. Was it hot? Was it cold? I believed it was raining, but the water couldn't penetrate me.

Words and thoughts had stopped. My ears were full of raven calls, but I didn't see them. I didn't bother to look. They were just cawing, calling out. Carrion eaters, dark birds of shadow, messengers to the dark gods, I had nothing to offer them. I had nothing to offer myself, only emptiness and defeat.

I found myself under a bush at the bottom of a steep grassy hill. The hill was littered with brilliant white boulders that at first I thought were sheep. The raven noise became human voices. A small crowd of townspeople was gathered at the top of the hill, and they were cackling more like a murder of crows, not ravens. I heard sharp squeals, deep bellows, and caw-caw-caw, like angry crows.

I stepped out from under the bush and rubbed my face with grimy hands. I felt the cold and wet of the day, and I shivered great uncontrollable shakes that went through my body in waves. At the top of the hill was a wooden cask. I could just make out that people seemed to be dancing around it and cackling with horrible laughter, like demons coming to witness. My mother must be up there somewhere.

Something black swooped down and hit the bush. I ducked, but it was only a raven that stood on one of the thicker branches, its weight causing it to sag perilously. I watched it with little interest as it tried to find something level to grasp.

Suddenly it floated up and, with one wing beat, plopped down heavily on my shoulder. I was surprised, but the emotion went away quickly. I was too raw to care. And now I was not alone. Its shining blue-black feathers were somehow comforting, and the claws gripping my shaking shoulder gave me substance. They were sharp and strong. *Drawing blood?* I wondered.

But I didn't care. It was a pain I could feel. My eyes had cleared, and now I could see my mum's crumpled body at the peak of the hill with the braver, or more foolish, of the townspeople dancing around her, sometimes kicking or other times punching. Some of them had baskets of garbage they threw at her.

A voice yelled, "That's enough!"

It was the executioner. He was a giant of a man with a hood over his head and bulging shoulder muscles coming out from his vest. There were dark holes cut where his eyes would be, and he looked like he was direct from the devil himself. Right behind him was Father Peck with his big silver cross waving in front of him, like a righteous banner or an avenging sword in the hands of a demon. It looked like the thing was burning into his hand and he was trying to fling it away. He threw it away again and again. I could almost see the smoke. I wished I could light the whole scene on fire.

The giant executioner lifted Mum from the pool her body made on the ground, and my shrunken raven's heart pinched in my chest. My whole body collapsed into itself. Brittle bones were all that was left holding me up, that and the raven on my shoulder.

He whispered, "What, what, what," into my ear. The air from his whisper seemed to revive me.

My mum was so small, just a wee wad of bone and gristle. Her beautiful, long black hair hung in strings and tangles, and I saw and felt the deadness. She was not there. The giant was surprisingly gentle as he lowered her into the cask. It could have been a dream. The pink-faced priest mumbled in a strange language and waved the horrible cross around the thing that had been my mum.

The executioner moved closer to the priest, saying something quietly, and the priest nodded his head. Then he mercifully put the cover on the cask, and with a mallet and nails, he hammered the lid on.

He began to pick up pointed wooden stakes and, one by one, hammered them into the side of the barrel. Not only wooden stakes, but large metal bolts honed to a shiny point and the broken blades of sabers were hammered into the barrel. Not a sound came from inside, even though many of the weapons found their mark. I knew. I felt each one until I crumpled to the ground on my hands and knees.

That was when the priest lifted the silver cross over his head, and the executioner tipped the barrel to its side and gave it a tremendous shove with his foot. The cask jumped off the edge of the hill and began a pitched and rolling ride down the face of the steep drop. It bounced off the sheep like boulders and flew into the air, only to crash down hard and resume its tumble, sometimes end over end. It flipped, bounced, and rolled.

I began to retch. My empty stomach had nothing to disgorge but its own bile, sickening, sour, and bitter. I spit and choked on my knees as the barrel careened toward me. My raven croaked and flew above me, circling and calling high in the air.

With a loud crash and the sound of splintering wood, the cask landed on a boulder in front of me. The barrel exploded into pieces. A cry went up from the crowd on top of the hill, and for several moments, they seemed frozen in place.

I wiped my mouth and nose, got up, and walked slowly to the ruins. Inside was the horror I expected. I fell to my knees. Reaching for her outstretched hand, I held it to my chest. Anything left of my heart froze over completely. No tears, only bile came. I swallowed it down and stood up.

As I turned around, I saw a horse and riders standing behind me. Dougal sat there. In front of him was Janet. She looked at the broken barrel and its bloody contents with a glow of triumph. A thin smile twitched on her lips. Dougal slumped with his head down behind her. He could not look at me. As the crowd began to run down the hill, it was Janet who gave leg to the horse, and it moved off.

"My mother was not a witch!" I screamed at them.

The black raven swooped down after the fleeing horse, calling, "What, what, what!"

"But I am," I said to myself.

7

A CALL FROM A QUEEN

I woke up facedown at the edge of the stream, not far from the cave. My eyes were sealed shut from the tears that dried on my face. My throat was raw, and my stomach felt like it was turned inside out. I crawled to the moss-covered bank and sucked a huge gulp of water down, only to double up in stabbing pain as it hit the insides of my dried-out stomach. Groaning as I lay down, I rested my head on a soft, mossy rock and curled up with my arms wrapped around my bent legs. It seemed to relieve the pain.

"Bernadette," a soft voice called. It sounded like a wind in the trees, playful and light. "Bernadette," it whispered again.

I pried my eyes open with grubby fingers.

"Splash some water on your face, dear."

The sound was like nothing I had ever heard, like music, birdsong, water trickling, breezes, and a crackling warm fire. I did as I was told and sat up, pushing with thin arms, my eyes still crusty, and my knees still pressed against my chest. I didn't want to let my tight stomach go. It would hurt.

Across the creek, only steps away, standing tall in a riding outfit that seemed to be made of spider webs flashing rainbow colors, was a queen. I knew it instinctively. She wore a cape the color of the forest that changed to browns and shades of greens as she moved. She took a step nearer. I wasn't sure if I should try to run or stand and curtsy.

In truth, I could do neither. So I sat and glared at her, daring her to harm me. I knew what she was, a Slig Maith, a dangerous and magical being.

"Do you know who I am, child?"

Her voice was so bright and sweet that it made me long to be her friend or to be hers. I would be happy to sit at her feet with her hand stroking the top of my head. Part of me would; the other part knew I should take care. She could kill me with a flick of her finger. The thought of being killed did not scare me though. I was angry, daring, and sick.

"No, Mum." My voice was tight and rasping. "But I have an idea. Won't you tell me?"

"I mean no harm, my beautiful girl. Please continue."

I let go of my stomach and used the nearby tree to pull myself up and stand. I was wavering and unstable, but it was better than groveling on the ground like a wounded pig.

"You are one of the Slig Maith for sure, the Good People, and I would not be surprised if you were their very queen," I said, boldly looking into her sparkling green eyes. Long, wild red hair framed her pure white, flawless face. She reminded me of my mum for some reason, and suddenly my fierceness dwindled. I teared up and took my eyes from hers.

"So intelligent. So observant."

She clapped her delicate hands together, and small bells tinkled in the air. She was trying to bewitch me. It felt like little tendrils of vapor were streaming out of her. How I could know this, I did not understand. I had never felt anything like it before.

"Woman," I said rudely, "what is it you want with me? I am not in condition to be your personal slave, and if you want to deal me a blow, yours will be the least of the blows I have received. But it would be the killing blow, I have no doubt. So just be done with it. I prefer not to live."

"Oh, my poor wee thing, I know what your blows have been. I've not come to finish you off, but to offer you revenge, to give you power, to make you a goddess in this world."

"Call off your bewitchment please. It will do you no good." My voice trailed off as the sickness of deep despair tried to overwhelm me. I was so tired.

She stood very straight as if she had been slapped. There was a rush of air through the trees. I watched her through lowered lids as her hands closed to fists. Her riding outfit of rainbow hues went cloudy gray, and her green cape got very dark, almost black. I could feel the danger behind her angry eyes, but I couldn't feel fear. I was too far gone.

I looked at the grasses and weeds growing around the stream and realized I was no more than one of them. I waited for her hand to pluck me up and throw me aside like a weed in a garden.

"You are very powerful indeed, but sadly you don't know it." She paced along the stream edge, a few steps up and a few steps down. "The courts of the Slig Maith want your help. You will be taught about your own power. If you agree, come with me."

I was so very tired. I knew I was in trouble. It must be a trick. The Good People just took what they wanted.

"I have no power." My voice came out in a growl.

Is she mocking me? I felt sick and dizzy, near to tears. *What could she possibly see in me, a child suddenly lost and alone who is probably near death?*

"But you do have power. I can't get near you unless you allow it. My own bewitchment magic is obvious to you. It doesn't penetrate. You have protection. We have skills to teach you."

"Why?" I could only stare blankly. Her words barely penetrated my understanding. Her talk of power only confused me. I was uniquely powerless. My family was gone.

"We need your help. We are losing a war that your realm has begun. Our numbers are dwindling. Our land is being destroyed. We foresee only complete disappearance or total inundation by your prolific race. We need help on this side more and more. You need help, your small life spark is almost out, and yet you can be a powerful mage and live forever."

There was fire in her voice now, like a forest fire starting to grow. It didn't scare me. I saw that my death was coming, and yet I was too weak to attract it or fight it.

"What are you saying? Are you saying I am a witch?"

"No, not a witch. We could teach you to know real magic, something very few of your kind ever know."

"You will train me to be a powerful witch? Do you know what they do to witches here?"

"There are no witches here! Our magic will keep you safe. We could give you magic. Wouldn't you like to kill those people who murdered your mother? We could give you that power. Come with me!" Her hair became flames flickering around her face.

I was too sick to be afraid. The thought of revenge hadn't seriously occurred to me. But I knew too much about the Slig Maith. "If I go with you, I will be bound to you forever." I almost toppled over. "No, I think not."

This fact was well known by everyone: people who went to the Slig Maith realm could not return. The Good People were never to be trusted.

"You would turn down more power than you can even think of?" She was clearly puzzled. "How is that possible for one of your race? Power is all you think about. Power and control," she said under her breath. Then with force, she stated, "You could become a queen here."

"But you need a king, madam." It was completely obvious. "Queens in this realm rule through their sons or not at all."

"Not if you have magic." She crossed her arms and stood squarely, eyes blazing.

The thought of hurting and even killing my mum's murderers began to grow in my mind. It felt like something I had to do. My anger pushed me to say, "All right then. I'll help you in return for my revenge. But I will not go with you. You must start my training and end it here in this realm. I will not go to yours where a year there might make fifty here. Unless it will be with freedom to return and a guarantee that I will return free. No ties. No big hunt for me."

The stories of encounters with the Good People were the tales told to children at bedtime by parents and grandparents. Everyone knew the name of some poor person or babe stolen, tricked, or killed by them.

"Ha!" She snorted. "Those men of the big hunt were fools. They left our realm without permission, and they were condemned to ride their horses forever around the earth because of their own misunderstanding. This could not happen to you. You, my dear, are much more than the mortal men from which you come. I agree with your conditions. We will start your training here. If and when you come to our realm, you will be free to leave."

She turned and swirled her cloak more closely around her shoulders. The sun was lowering, and the colors of her clothing, earlier as bright as they could be, remained muted. The cloak stayed the dark green it had turned. As she moved, I could see guards on horses. They were just visible behind a gauzy film sparkling in the air at the edge of my world and hers. And I wouldn't swear to it, but the beautiful animals they rode were the illusive and dangerous Each Visge, water horses. Meat eaters they were. Large canines hung from their mouths where no bit and bridle were ever fitted. No one I knew had ever seen one, but everyone knew a story about one.

"My queen!" I called. "When does the training start?"

She turned in a swirl of colors. "It has started. Be aware! Be present. Now go to your den and eat, sleep, and be strong!"

The Each Visge parted, and a pure white steed stepped forward. She leapt to its back as if she were merely a feather, and without a sound, the animals with their riders followed her into the mire.

As soon as they disappeared, I broke into a sweat; wracked by spasms of shivering so strong they almost knocked me down. I leaned more solidly against the tree.

I had just stood up to a queen of the Good People. *What had gotten into me?* We called them the Good People just to keep them happy. Their tempers and magical powers were well known to all. According to Mum, they fell out of heaven when the devil created a big hole and jumped out. God didn't fix the hole right away, so a lot of angels kept falling out. When he did fix it, he didn't bring any of them back up. Nobody knew why. There were good ones, and there were bad ones.

I balanced myself on stiff legs and made my halting way to the cave.

I had to crawl on hands and knees to get inside because, when I bent over to get in, I toppled down like a newborn foal, all legs. I needed food. I was sure I was going to die because I couldn't remember if there was anything in the cave to eat.

What is death anyway? My da had just disappeared. One morning, he was there, his cheery, too talkative self, and that afternoon he was gone. I never saw a body. Mum screamed like a banshee. We all cried, but I never quite believed he was dead. I saw and felt the death of my mum. *Would that happen to me? Or would I just disappear and someone would say I was dead?*

I lifted my head as I crawled through the crack. By this time, I was so accustomed to my own personal light in dark places that the fact that I could see in that cave didn't even cause me to wonder. But what I saw surely, it did!

A small man was crouching over a fire. He was dressed in shabby green breeks down to his knees and a vest. His bare skin was like tree limbs covered in rough bark. The sight of him and the smell of food cooking filled me with wonder. In total shock, I opened my mouth to yell and fell over. I could have been struck dead for all I knew.

When I awoke, I was on my pallet covered in blankets, and the Broonie, for that was what he was, leaned over me with a spoon smelling of herbs and maybe meat. I gasped, and he shoved a small amount of broth into my gaping mouth. It was so delicious that I might have been in heaven.

If you had to die to get there, I could tell that it hadn't happened because the cave walls were reeling. I was shaking so hard that only the Broonie's calm hand on the spoon got the liquid into my mouth. From that moment on, I loved that Broonie. His name was Murray.

8

MURRAY

I was sick for many days. Whether for lack of eating or my mother's horrible death and the hate that brewed in me, there was no telling. That little brown Broonie tended me diligently. There was not a need he left unfulfilled. I tossed and turned in fever so hot that my own sweat poured out to cool me. My dreams were of the horrendous barrel careening from rock to rock in a never-ending fall while I felt every blade and crashing blow, rolling and spinning as if dizzying pain were all there was left of my world.

The hate in me grew until I felt the wee, ugly walnut of my heart burn like a coal in my chest. I did not want to live. Revenge wasn't enough to make living worthwhile. Then I would open my eyes to the soft light of the cave. I could hear and see the crackling bright flames of the fire in its circle and little Murray bent over a pot of steaming food, a cup of tea in one hand. He would instantly know I was back from the fate of my dreaming and appear by my side with a bowl and a spoon, cooling down the hot liquid with his own breath.

There came a time when a far-off mumbling woke me, trembling and soaked in my own sweat. When my eyes opened, there was Murray sitting comfortably on a small rock with one thin leg crossed over the other. He was reading out loud. I recognized the sounds as Latin.

"Am I dying?" My voice came out crackly and hoarse.

He was reading my last rites, like they did over the place where they said they put my da's body.

"Hmm? That's an odd question, deary. I dina' think yas anywhere near that endin'." His voice was soft and high.

Is he a he or a she? I didn't even know if there were lady Broonies. All I knew about them was, if you kept them happy, they worked with you. If you made them mad, they became Boggarts and would make your life miserable.

I took a swallow. "I never hear Latin unless some priest be reading it somewhere and lastly over my da's grave."

"Ah well," said Murray.

It could be a girl's name, I guessed.

"I'm readin' ye Latin so's you'll larn it by and by." He put the thick parchment down and got up to feel my forehead. "I'm thinkin' you've broke that fever and you'll be up and around in no time." He filled a bowl with the broth and gave me a spoonful as I lay there. I had gathered all of the blankets I had around me and was feeling on the better side of bad.

"Might I have a bit of bread?" A very deep hunger came over me. "A piece of cheese, a bite of meat, a potato, turnip, or onion?" My stomach turned, and an angry growl erupted from it as if it had been denied food for longer than it wanted to wait.

Murray turned his back for a moment, and when he turned to me again, there was a very small piece of light wheat bread, the kind of bread served to the lairds and the people of the manse. So soft and chewy, it felt unreal in my mouth. I detected a delicate fine flavor of salt and honey and wheat milled to perfection. After two bites, the morsel was gone.

"That's it," said Murray. "You'll be throwin' it back out if thars anymore. Chew it up good afore ya swallow, or that cranky stomach of yers will be revoltin'."

I had no knowing of the time while I was sick in my cave. There was no light to follow the day to the night, and I spent most of my time in a fevered haze until the day I ate some bread. From then on, my days or nights consisted of sleeping, some eating, hearing a droning voice speaking Latin, and sleeping.

But there did come a day when Murray said, "Tis time now, lass, for ye to be going outside. Summer is on the wane, the day is fine and warm, and you need light and exercise."

That made sense, but the doing of it was the hard part. Murray was half my height. He didn't seem strong enough to lift me to my feet. I was wrong. He bent down and picked me up with his sticklike arms as if I were a wee bairn. My feet practically dragged on the floor, but I didn't have to crawl out of the cave on hands and knees.

It was a beautiful Highland day. The warm sun felt so good on my grimy white skin. Murray had tried to keep me clean, but I could smell my own rankness.

He put me gently down by the trickling stream and handed me a rag. "Ye can start by washin' yaself."

"Have you got a bit of soap? I brought a few bars that my mum made ..." I began.

"Never ye fear," he said. A heavily used chunk of it appeared on the ground in front of me.

Seeing it there made shivers run up and down my body. In fact, I would swear I felt a wavering, like a breeze, in the body of little Murray, but he really hadn't moved. I stared at the soap and then looked over at him. He was standing there with his brown arms crossed in a tattered smock with his grimy pants covering down to the tree burls that were his knees. It was hard to read a Broonie's face, but I was sure it was smug.

"What did ya do?" I said, gulping down a breath. "Was it magic?"

"What do ya think, missy?" His thin lips parted in an infrequent smile as he looked down his long nose at me. "Did ya notice somthin' queer? Or feel somthin' change? Mayhaps I jus' trode it at ya."

"No, you did not throw it. Something changed. And it was you. I saw or felt a wavering of your body. Was it magic?"

"You'll do." The thin smile was gone from his face. But his arms were crossed tighter than ever as if he were trying to keep something from getting out. "You'll do." He repeated it more softly as if his thoughts were more important.

"What!" My voice was hardly a whisper, but I could feel some strength coming back as I sat cross-legged in the sun. The sound of the creek was a trickle of merriment beside me.

"Get cleaned up," he commanded. "When yer finished, get yerself into the cave. We'll 'ave a right proper dinner." As he turned to go, I saw another waver and felt a little breeze. A clean smock and breeks, neatly folded, appeared next to me. I couldn't help but yell, "Hey! What!"

He ignored me and trudged away. My stomach made such a roiling growl that it would have scared me if I did not know it was my own body. The thought of real food made me want to hurry, but the smell of reek on my clothes and skin made me take care with the washing. I even washed my hair, which was growing out and down to my shoulders. The water was chill, but the day was warm, and the sun glinted on my wet skin. I felt something on me or in me loosening up a wee bit, like the pure flowing water cleaned not only the outside but opened a space on my inside. Despite myself, I felt a little worry fall away. For the time being, I looked forward to something, mostly food, but I was curious to know about magic.

The queen had said, "Be aware, be present, and be strong." Now I could.

The sun was below the trees as I made my way on wobbling, clean legs to the cave. The Broonie had swept and cleaned the entrance. Some clean fresh straw was strewn on the floor. I was sure it was in case I had to crawl. I was not wanting to dirty my new clean breeks. I managed to make the passage on both feet, which was a fulfilling feeling. I felt like smiling when I entered the cave, but my face wasn't ready yet.

I stood, slightly swaying. I was wanting to be happy, but tears of pain, heart pain, interrupted, and I let them flow down my face and sobbed. Through the watery haze, I could see Murray pointing to a small wooden stool next to the fire, and I moved slowly toward it as I wiped my eyes with my clean shirtsleeves.

That night, we had such a feast as I could have only imagined. And I could have eaten much more, but the caring Murray stopped me. He put small morsels of rabbit meat, mushrooms cooked in fat, and fresh greens from the forest on my dish. There were some nuts and a small piece of that fine wheat bread, all to be swallowed down with long draughts of watered ale, a healing beverage for sure.

"Don' go gulpin' ye food, me lassie. Mayhaps ya's needin' some manners, aye? In fact, I'm thinkin' that be so."

He peered at me so hard and long that I began feeling a slight uncomfortable feeling. The bite remaining in my mouth went down hard, a rock squeezing down my neck until it dropped into my stomach. I grabbed my cup and quickly took a drink to make the landing easier.

"I once served a most cultured lady," he continued.

"What happened?" I interrupted.

"She thought I needed a new smock, and with the offerin' of it, I had ta leave. Them's the rules. Too bad too. We had a right good life together." As he stared into the fire, his eyes got glassy with the memory.

I felt a little guilty then. He must be longing for comforts and the warmth of carpets and a fireplace.

"I know the rules," I muttered softly. I would not say them to him.

The fact was that the Broonie must leave a house if the master or mistress offered him clothing. It was such a simple thing. Everyone knew that.

"Maybe lairds and ladies don't know the rules?" I offered.

"Mayhaps they don'," he said cheerily. "Not to worry. We'ins here be havin' a good life. Broonies like me always do. No worries. An' you lookin' better an' better. In fact, I dare say you's gonna be a proper lady a'fore I get through wit ya. Never mind."

The small platter on my lap suddenly vanished. The cup in my hand filled with water, and on my lap, a bite of hard white cheese appeared.

"Dessert!" he said with a smile.

I jumped when the dish went away. I was convinced I would never get used to the comings and goings of magic, but it fired my imagination anyway.

"Are you going to teach me that?" I asked. My eyes were still wide as I fingered the bit of cheese. "Is it real?"

"Aye, it is as real as any piece of cheese fer sure. Go on, you've already eaten the bits from conjurin' like I do. Did they taste real?"

"They were real," I said slowly because they entered my stomach, and before that, my teeth chewed, and my mouth tasted. "Are you gonna teach me?" I repeated. I couldn't control the wonderment of the possibility.

"Yeah, you'll do. You'll make a right good Broonie, ya will." A little smile slowly creeped up his face, and one eye raised. He wanted to know how I would take this news.

"I don't want to be a Broonie," I said, not looking at him. "I have other things I have to do, you know."

How could I ever become a Broonie? I would never be tall. That was true, but I would always have white, soft skin and black hair.

"Never fear, little missy! I be teasin' ye. Wot am I gonna do wit yas? I'm goin'ta train ya up sos ya will be the most beautiful killin' machine in this realm and mayhaps the other. An' I'm goin' ta larn ya how to be a proper lady. Yer dear mum will be so proud o' you. An' yer da too. When I'm done, ol' Queenie of the rainbow cape will beg for yer help, and you will be able to choose yea or nea. Ya will be fearsome strong. I promise."

He jumped off his wee chair and came over to me. With his sticklike fingers, he took my hands in his, and looking fiercely into my eyes, he said, "I so promise."

9

LIU (LOU) SHEN

Murray had promised he'd make a lady of me, and he was trying his darndest in the year and a half we had spent together. He fiddled with the way I talked and taught me how to prepare meals, politely greet guests, curtsy to kings and lords, and sew. He even taught me to knit so I might have a trade at the new knitting business that had come to Forresgem. I was mostly interested in magic of course, but he insisted there would be time enough. Reading and writing were the magic I learned first.

I learned the language of our neighbors and enemies, the Brits, and soon enough I knew the alphabet and was reading and understanding Latin. I couldn't actually speak it, but somehow the written word translated to Brits and Scots in my head. The Broonie showed me handwritten scrolls and parchments with Latin on one side and English on the other. He had a printed copy of the "Scotichronicon," which was sometimes quite boring but was the history of Scotland with our first

Scottish king, Robert de Bruce, recorded in it. As my reading improved, so did my speech, and I soon transformed my peasant dialect into one more suitable to a learned lady of the manse.

None of this mattered to me at all. Peasantry had never bothered me. I didn't yearn for anything better. Now that I was better, all I wanted was my revenge. I dreamt about it at night and thought about it in spare moments when I was awake. Sometimes a quiet moment came during knitting or sewing, and I fantasized about sticking a knitting needle into Janet's throat while she slept. I'd make my way back to the cave in the dark and prepare for the next revenge murder: the sheriff, the fat priest, or Dougal.

I thought that I might let Dougal live. He was the only one who knew what he had done and had any feelings about it. His revenge would be to live with those feelings. His own personal hell realm was right here on the top of the ground. I would send the rest of them to Dante's inferno.

One autumn day, we were out in the woods, not far from the cave. I was washing out some clothes in a pan near the creek and listening to Murray natter on about where to find the best mushrooms. He paced back and forth with his hands behind his back, and I got the feeling he was very tense. Every now and then, he would stop and look out into the woods just for a moment and then turn around and continue his pacing. That day was cool and crisp, and small animals were scurrying around, looking for food to store for later, a sure sign winter was coming.

Needless to say, it was a bit of a shock to find an unusual man looking at us from the other side of the creek. I had not heard a thing of his movement through the woods. Murray must have been so tense that he hadn't either. We both stared.

"I'm looking for Ravenheart," the stranger said in a clear voice with a slight accent. He was obviously not Scottish or Brit.

Since Murray didn't answer, I sat up straight and said, "This is Raven Heart Forest."

"Not what I mean," he said.

Then Murray came to action. "You have found Ravenheart. Now what do you want?"

That was a little blunt from Murray, not very polite at all. *Who was this Ravenheart?*

The strange man bowed very deeply from each bone in his back, one at a time, starting from the bottom until his head hung low. When he came back up, he straightened from the bottom of his back, with each bone rising up until his head was perfectly placed on top of his neck and shoulders. I had never seen anyone so in control of his body. We didn't bow like that here, not unless a person of high status like the laird of the manse and his lady came near to us. That almost never happened, so I was very surprised. I looked around quickly just to make sure King James hadn't snuck up among us.

Right then, my raven flew up and landed heavily on my shoulder. He didn't even give me a warning, but I was pretty used to him by now. I gave him a glare out the corner of my eye.

"You? You are Ravenheart?" A momentary look of surprise grabbed at the man's face as his slit-like eyes stared into mine.

I looked over at Murray for some help. He didn't look at me, just at the stranger.

"I am Liu Shen, at your service."

I was trying to get up off my knees when the big bird on my shoulder sunk his weight down and then leapt up. It almost knocked me right down into my washing. He flew low, right at Liu, who didn't move a muscle. The glistening black raven flapped once and just cleared Liu's head as it flew up into a tree where it watched, clucked, and rolled its golden eyes.

"You called," he said quietly.

"I did, sir." Murray was standing right at the edge of the creek. His toes were almost in the water. "I called ye," he repeated. "We are in need of a teacher, one who knows the secrets of alchemy."

I felt a stirring, like bees buzzing and bumping into the palms of my hands. I lifted them to look just as an apple settled into them. It was perfect: bright and shiny red, large with juicy promise. I almost threw it to the ground. But I was used to Murray's conjuring and held on to it. My mouth and eyes opened wide as I looked at Murray for help.

"Like this?" said Lou as he smiled. A neat and perfect row of white teeth showed briefly between his lips.

"That's it," said Murray with a chuckle. "Eat it, lass. Tell us wots ya think."

I took one giant bite, and the rich, sweet nectar of that apple's juice flooded my mouth. I chewed slowly and swallowed.

"Oh, Murray," I stammered. "What was that word I learned the other day? Food of the gods? Ambrosia? This is that, food for the gods."

He nodded as he looked at me. One of those thin smiles creeped onto his thin lips, "Come then," he said, looking at the stranger. "Our home is yer home."

Lou crossed the creek, and he and Murray grasped elbows in greeting as if they were old friends. The raven shrieked and snapped its wings. *Who would have guessed? Ravenheart was me.*

We called him Lou, and he was the strangest man I had ever seen. His black hair was as dark as night, pulled back and braided so it spun down his back longer than any woman's. On a cold day, he would wrap that braid around his neck at least four times to keep himself warm. Single hairs sprouted randomly from his face as if testing the surface for a future beard.

His most unusual features were his eyes. They seemed to always be half-closed. They weren't the rounded eyes of us in Scotland. They were more like thin crescent moons. They made his round, brown face so unusual that people might back away in fright if they saw him at the market. Once I got used to that strange face, I didn't even notice that he was different. He said he was from somewhere very far away called Ming.

Murray's teaching continued, and now Lou added to my training. The very next morning, he woke me up before daylight.

"Please follow me," he said. "Bring a blanket." The tone of his voice didn't give me any room for complaint. I got up to see what he wanted.

Wrapped in my coarse wool blanket, I stepped outside into a chilly night. A black cloud covered the stars, but my little light was with me as I stood in front of Lou, not far from the cave opening and the blackberry bush.

"I want to show you your mind." There was no smile on his serious, strange face. He was not teasing. "Please kneel. Sit on your legs, like this." In one smooth move, he sunk to the ground, legs bent under him.

It was not so simple for me. But after wrapping myself in the blanket, I was able to copy his sitting. I was hunched over with the blanket pulled tightly over my head and shoulders, but it couldn't stop my shivering.

"Back straight," he demanded.

I immediately sat up.

"Try to relax. Relax everything. Until you do this, this position will be difficult."

I tried. But the chill air kept me tense. I was wracked with shivers, and I could hardly sit still. Soon my legs began to prickle, and pain like a fire burned inside them.

So began the torture that Lou called *watching the mind*.

"This is very easy. Watch your mind think. Don't think for it. Watch as it thinks. Someday your thoughts will stop. Tell me when that happens." He got up. "You stay. I say when to stop. Thank you." He went back into the cave.

That first morning of sitting pushed me to the limits of my sanity. I hated Lou. I thought our meeting was a mistake. *He must be evil, maybe a Slig Maith monster.* I moved around on my seat. I could not keep my knees bent with my weight on top of them for long. I wondered if I should get up and walk around. I didn't think so. But I couldn't sit like that for long. *Had he forgotten me? How could I watch my thoughts when I was in so much pain?*

Just when I couldn't take it anymore, Lou came out. It was a gray dawn. I was angry.

"You are not relaxed," he said, looking at me with merry eyes.

I glared back. My knees and ankles were crippled. I was sure I'd never walk again.

"This practice is very important. It gives focus, clarity, and relaxation. You cannot understand now, but as days go by, you will know what I say is truth, and you will make this sitting basic to life." He reached down and took my arm, gently tugging me to my feet. "Small steps. You need to practice this style of sitting. In the cave, sit like this when you can. Practice. Practice."

The sitting did get easier. Watching the mind was another thing. It thought up ways to kill and devised plans for my revenge. Often if I followed it into my past, my lost sister and mother's death brought me to tears.

Lou seemed to think that was good. "You must feel the pain. It is in your body. You must let it out."

To me, crying was being sorry for nothing. I would let my mind indulge this for a short time but cut it off before I got to the crying part. Lou said it would keep coming up and I should not be afraid of it. But crying didn't feel good. I had already cried so much. I wanted to be done with it. Crying could not be allowed.

After sitting long enough to feel like my legs were burning off at the knees, Lou would help me up, and I would hobble around until the pain went away. Then we would walk the few steps to the trickling creek and just stand. Lou called it tree posture, standing like I was holding a tree. My arms were out in front like an embrace, only round.

During this practice, I began to hear the forest. The trees were speaking. I could not make out any words. It was more like a feeling in my body, like a surging of something inside. The trees were perfectly happy. They had no cares. In fact, they were blissful. I envied their peace. Rightness for me would not come until my revenge was complete.

Lou also began training my body. We did some really silly moves to warm up in the mornings. We stood with our feet slightly spread and swung our arms from side to side with the turning of our bodies. We walked around in a small circle, and Lou taught me how my body should line up, from the ground to the top of my head. There were so many things to pay attention to, not to mention the new words.

He said the word *energia* came from Latin. It was the closest thing to what he was talking about, a kind of internal force. He said *heaven energia* pulled the body in an upward pattern while *earth energia* pushed down. This happened at the same time, and so the forces were always going up and down.

My job was to learn to feel the *energia* in the body and then learn to use or enhance them. The early training moves were very slow. They gradually got more and more complex with the addition of other body parts and the *energia* flows.

"Try to keep your mind still and just feel," he coached.

Try was the important word because, try as I might to keep my mind still, I could not. I found myself wondering if I were doing the move right, what Murray was making for breakfast, and why I needed to read Latin when I already spoke Brits and Scots. Stupid things would catch my attention, even some important things like the best ways to kill the sheriff. *Maybe I should just maim him and leave him alive.*

I thought up revenge murders and how I would escape from the deed, leaving no trace. Watching the mind didn't make sense to me. I wasn't watching. I was participating in planning and dreaming, and soon the watcher was the doer of the thoughts, forgotten in all the action and excitement.

I did enjoy the physical movements, and it didn't take too long before I came to realize this practice had to do with fighting. That caught my interest, and I began to watch Lou a little more closely. He didn't talk very much. I mimicked his movements. Walking around the circle was not just walking. It was gliding along the surface of the ground. The foot going out felt the layout of the land. The foot in the back spent was kept weighted with the body. The front foot would reach out, set down, and pull the body forward. It was a strange way to walk. There was no jaunty up-and-down action, like regular walking. I felt like one of the big Highland wildcats moving along. My feet gripped the ground as they moved.

I felt lighter than ever when I discovered that sinking into the ground with *energia* producing upward movement. Like when a raven got ready to fly, it would sink down before taking off. On the other hand, I could get as heavy as a boat anchor or stuck as a fence post. All it took was the intention of my mind and the correct alignment of my body. These skills might be useful in combat.

One day as we walked around the circle, Lou said, "You must pay notice to the ten thousand things."

A small sample of the things I was learning began with relaxing. I learned to tuck my lower back and let my head float up. I was to let my shoulders relax down, yet hold one arm and hand up to look at the opponent through fingers shaped like a "tiger's mouth." The other arm would ward the front of the body in a rounded yet relaxed way. All of this was in a fluid roundness.

With an aligned body, Lou said, our body's *qi*, or life force, was connected. The *qi* flowed like water, giving us strength and power. I thought I would never grasp all the small things that the body needed to do to allow this force and power. I was often tense in my jaw or unbalanced in my body, out of alignment.

Winter progressed. I was into my fifteenth year. My menses finally came. I knew about them from my mum, and so I tried to do what she had done, but I really couldn't remember. The Broonie knew what to do. He brought a basket of clean rags and said to tie something like a bandage between my legs onto a length of rope around my waist.

He also said, "Maybe it's time to wear a dress."

"I can't wear a dress just yet, Murray. I'm in the middle of a new gua, and there are kicks," I whined. "Plus, it's cold out there. Can I wait until spring at least?"

"Wot's a gua?" he asked, his eyes wide with curiosity.

"Oh, in Lou's language, a gua is a series of fighting moves. He is teaching me hand-to-hand combat."

It felt so good to say that. I had always wanted to fight, mostly dragons, but this was a first step. Magic would take care of the rest.

"Hmm ... Well, I guess 'e knows wot e's doin'. Don know wot that has to do wit alchemy, but I knows it would na' hurt ye to know some fightin'. Ya might need it fer sure."

"And besides that, it's fun." I needed something fun.

"But ya's so small. How in ta werld you goin' to fight anyone?" He was puzzled.

"My size will confuse any man fer sure. Lou says that soft beats hard in every fight. He's showing me how to use life force."

"Ah! That makes sense. It's magic fer sure. Good fer ya, girlie. You practice an' practice. I want to see ya beat Lou at a match someday!" He beamed. For Murray, it had to be magic.

"Och! Beat my own teacher? Murray! I don't think I could be that good."

"Try, dearie. You try and make a Broonie happy." A wee tear formed in his right eye.

There was no more talk about dress wearing. Murray had insisted that I learn to make my own clothes so I had several of my own making packed away in a box, and they would stay there. I made Lou and me hats and gloves for the cold winters. We wore knitted leggings and arm warmers that I made too, so we continued our practice outside in all weather except the drenching downpours and blizzards. The cave stayed warm and dry, and we had plenty of everything we needed.

I dove into all of my lessons with intensity. Lou was often telling me, "Relax your face." I tried to remember to relax it, but I was still thinking long and hard about the killing I had to do.

He began to tell me more and more about *energia*. It was something that was everywhere and could be used by a wise person.

"Or a mage?" I asked him.

"A mage is just a wise person," he said.

We were sitting in the cave on the small chairs next to the fire. I was finding my chair slightly uncomfortable and contemplating the floor. Murray threw some tea into the kettle, and while it boiled, its scent slowly filled the cave.

He always said, "There be nothing like the feel and smell of cooking."

Lou went on, "This next lesson is hard to understand. You need to discover a feel for it. It is that nothing, not even invisible things like thoughts, are without connection. You will notice that, when you watch your mind, your thoughts depend on other thoughts as they arise, one after another. The world and everything of the world is made of tiny particles that we can't see, feel, hear, or taste," he said seriously. "Relax your face, child."

I tried, but my brain was so furiously working to understand that I could feel my brows pinched together and my mouth in a stiff frown. Then my brain just stopped and gave up, and my face let go in a sudden relaxation. I felt a shift in my body as all of my tension released. A wide and brilliant space opened up in my mind. I was lost in there. It felt really good to be so spacious and still, but a wee bit of me, still there inside the space, became afraid, and it screamed out, "No!" I almost fell out of my chair.

Lou looked at me with a big smile on his face. Murray was curious but didn't move from the fire, leaving Lou to continue as if nothing had happened.

"The smallest particles of these tiny particles are everywhere. They create us. We eat and breathe them, and if we are very wise, we can use them to create things."

"Is that alchemy?" I didn't want to lose track of the topic of magic so I let the experience go.

"Not alchemy the way today's scientists try to turn lead into gold. You might say it's making something from nothing. Just know that there are the smallest particles and that is all you need to create. That and space."

Without warning, I felt like I was full of the smallest particles, and they were bashing against each other out of control. Some were even escaping and flying off me into the cave. My skin was crawling, and below the skin, there was a prickling and roiling. Deep inside me, it was like a sea of raging particles all slamming against each other and swirling around, looking for space.

Lou saw my discomfort. "It is good you can feel this, but you need to know that inside you there is more space than particles. Everything made of the smallest particles is also made of infinite space. The smallest particles create what we see and feel as things. They are connected within a vast space. Nothing exists on its own. Everything is dependent on something else. Can you understand this?" he asked with his eyebrows raised.

He looked at me intently, and I could feel a gentle force move from him. The swirling, itchy particles stopped moving within me. At least I didn't feel them so strongly.

"Infinite. That means it goes on forever, but how is it possible to have a thing, a body, with infinite space? I don't get that." I shook my head slowly back and forth, looking at the flames of the fire as they leaped and plunged, disappearing and reemerging from the coals in a happy dance of heat.

"Don't think too much, girl. Relax your face," he told me with a smile of affection. "Anything else?"

"I think I understand connection and how everything is dependent. Is that the word?"

"Yes! Brilliant!" He laughed and clapped his hands. "Go on." He leaned forward. His eagerness was clear, and it gave me courage.

"Look at a chair." I shifted in my seat a little, and it creaked loudly. "It's made from a tree. But it had a lot of things happen to it before it became a chair. The tree had to start from a seed that found the right location to grow. It was dependent on earth, rain, and sun, not to mention air. Then time. Then someone, a man, had to see it and think *chair* or something like that. Maybe he thought *warming fire* or *furniture*. I don't know, but someone cut down the tree and made the chair.

"The chair could have been something else, but someone made the legs, the seat, and the back and called it chair. At every stage, there was something or someone that it depended on to make it a chair. Right now, it is dependent on four legs and a seat, and we who sit on it or call it *chair* are probably part of its dependent arising also."

"Very good!" he yelled and clapped again. He jumped off his seat, grabbed little Murray's hands, and swung him around in the air as if he were a child.

All the while, Murray laughed and said, "See! She'll do! She'll do!"

I smiled to see them having fun. "But..." I could feel my face tighten up. I was thinking hard. "I don't understand what this has to do with the smallest particles. Are we talking about magic? What are the smallest particles dependent on? I am confused."

Murray and Lou stopped their carousing and looked at me, still holding each other's hands. Murray dropped Lou's hands and stepped back, grabbing the frayed edges of his vest like he was getting ready for a speech.

"That's an excellent couple of questions, sir. What say ye in answer?" Then he went to the fire to pour the hot tea into cups.

Lou picked up two and came back to his chair, handing me a cup.

"Thank you," I said in my most intelligent, ladylike accent.

"These, indeed, are most intelligent questions." Lou very daintily took a sip of hot tea. "I tell you that everything is dependent on the smallest particles. The smallest particles are dependent on mind, and that is magic. This I leave for another lesson. Relax your face, please."

10

MAGIC

Snow and rain intermingled with days of damp chill that spring. I spent much of my time in the cave. I was beginning to settle into my sitting practice. Space, big and open, accompanied me frequently, but an underlying current of agitated *qi* was flowing through me. I had bouts of restless moving where my insides felt like they were bubbling over and needed to get out.

My body was changing, and before my eyes, I was turning into a very near duplication of my own mum. I had the same fair skin and the raven black hair with auburn lights. Wisps of it always escaped her cowl and floated like dark clouds around her high cheekbones and merry eyes. Whenever I found myself tucking wayward strands of my own dark locks away, I thought of her. She was always neat and tidy; I was more apt to be disheveled.

I had never heard of *energia* or *qi* before I met Lou. He said we could feel it when we were tired or happy, and that was all he meant. When we were tired, it was low, not moving much. When we were happy, it flowed up, and movement was easier. But that wasn't all he meant.

It didn't take long for me to notice the light flowing movement of *qi* in my body. There was a down and an up as well as an in and an out. Focusing on the down *qi* movement made me heavy. I didn't gain weight or get bigger. I stuck to the ground better. It meant that it was harder for someone to move me. When I focused on the up flows, I became lighter and faster. When these ups and downs combined, spiraling *energia* occurred, and I became less of a target for my opponent. I could become unmovable, or I could become uncatchable. All occurred with the speed of thought.

My fighting practice got harder, and I learned more about *energia*. It had everything to do with meeting the opponent relaxed and open, allowing our *qi* to become one. I realized I could influence my opponent by using the down, up, in, and out energy flows of my body. Lou showed me how I could transform my movements to create the feeling of wind, fire, earth, metal or water. Each element had its own forces, but harnessing them was easier said than done.

When I got my practice right, my mind was clear, and I did not need to know where Lou's body began and ended. There was no separation between us. My body was his body. We moved in harmony with no thought. I knew, through my body, when a flowing force like water or a heavy earth force was coming from him. When this happened, I could block a punch or resist a pull, and I could feel where I might give a punch or pull. This feeling lasted only the briefest of moments, but in that moment, a fluidness came out of our movement.

When I was out of the moment, there was no connection to Lou. My mind wandered, and I felt unbalanced. I had no connection to my own body. When I lost the connection, he would be merciless with a punch or a slap. At first, these attacks shook me up, and I would not be able to respond. Gradually I learned to relax and return to our harmony.

We did a kind of grappling practice, pushing, pulling, or somehow getting the opponent to move his feet or fall. Sometimes we stood in front of each other, just barely touching one wrist to the other. My right wrist to his right wrist together, making a circle in front of our stationary bodies. It was give-and-take. First I pushed lightly, and then I retreated my wrist as he pushed.

Gradually we began to apply more pressure, use our qi to find a weak spot, and then press an attack. I never won. But I could feel Lou as a slippery kind of force, able to hide way inside himself or to flood outward. With the minutest of touches, he could pick me up and drop me like a wave on the ocean. He assured me that I could do this also.

"Relax down. Relax face. Feel. Don't imagine."

At the end of one session, Lou put a hand on my sweaty shoulder and said, "A warrior steps aside but does not give way. Never yield to the opponent. Use all your skill."

"I have no skill," I said.

"You have more skill than you think. Please go cleanup. When you are finished, sit quietly and meditate on what it means to step aside."

"Yes," I said with a bow.

My bowing always surprised me, done without a thought. Lou seemed to command that kind of respect. But he often bowed to Murray. In fact, we were all bowing to each other. It was nothing ornate, just slight bows or tips of the head. It felt right.

I spent the rest of the afternoon sitting outside. Once I finally quieted my mind, I felt the spaciousness of awareness and filled it with stepping aside. Then I was off on a tangent about warriors, fighting, and killing. I saw Lou in my mind's eye, fighting a ferocious demon and killing anyone who got in his way. He didn't step aside. He plunged ahead with speed and deadly blows. He could decapitate someone with the palm of his hand, using metal energy as clean and sharp as an axe. His long braid wreathed out behind him like a snake, always evading the demon as if it had a mind of its own.

Then the demon became the sheriff, and Lou killed him with a flat hand full of spiraling energy like a tornado to the chest. Then it was the priest, whose red eyes and sharp, pointed teeth dripped blood. He was too slow, and Lou kicked him on the side of the head and killed him with a crushing blow to his throat.

Just as I was getting to Janet, I noticed. Once again, I was not watching my thoughts. I was making up fantastic stories with Lou as the hero. *What am I doing?* Abruptly my fantasy disappeared. I was left thinking what a waste my meditation time had been, uselessly filled with fantasy stories. It was hard to let them go. They felt so good. I wanted to be there watching while Lou vanquished all of my enemies with his skill. *Would I ever be close to skilled?*

Off I went into my thoughts. My mind was not quiet but very noisy. Once again, I caught myself and all fantasy stopped. I was so disgusted that I got up and went into the cave. *I quit. My mind is out of control. I'm just no good.*

Lou was on the rocky ledge inside, practicing fighting moves with a long staff. He was so flowing and fast in his movements. It was beautiful. I could feel his *qi* spiraling in and out as he parried and attacked an unseen opponent. He seemed to float in a field of clarity that I sensed covered him like a bubble everywhere he went.

"I'll never be able to do that," I mumbled to myself. Tears began to fill my eyes as I realized I was a failure.

Lou came to a halt, saluting his invisible opponent with a bow.

"A true warrior is never a cruel killer, murdering her enemies without a thought." He walked up to me. "Her ultimate opponent is her own self. The only demons to conquer are inside. Did you discover anything about yielding? What does it mean to step aside?"

"No." I sobbed. "I only discovered that I am a failure at all things." I bowed my head in defeat and let my tears drain to the ground.

"Please." He motioned for me to follow him to the smooth surface of the bedrock where he had been practicing. He leaned the staff against the wall and faced me, ready to grapple.

I wiped my eyes and met his gaze, meeting his challenge by touching the back of his hand with my own, a ward-off position. At that moment, I could feel the field of clarity that I had sensed in him engulf me. It felt spacious and open. My body seemed to puff up, like new flower petals opening on a spring day.

He smiled. "Now you do that."

I cleared my mind, entering what was, to me, a bubble of clarity. It surrounded me in a sphere of empty space. It was not visible; it could only be felt. Looking at Lou sent part of the bubble onto him. I could feel my own field of clarity now included him. It took only a moment. He must have been helping me somehow, but I felt a sense of knowing him. This was more than harmonizing. That was when he made his first move, a pull down.

My body responded without my mind. I sank inside myself. I took a step, and the sinking energy released out, spinning. It was not a spin that could be seen, but I could feel it arising from the bottom of my feet and spiraling through my body until, finding release in my arm, it slammed into Lou's shoulder.

My arm, backed by my whole body, crashed into him with the minutest touch, but the impact was huge. He absorbed it. With my newfound clarity, I could feel, like water seeping down a crack, where he had an opening in his *energia*. I moved to that space on his body. Lou filled it just in time, but as he did, another space opened up.

I aimed my body there with an attack. Over and over again, he would let me feel an opening. I'd make my attack, and he would almost relent. He'd come back again and again, sometimes a nudge other times a pull, a punch, a slap, or a kick. His whole body was a weapon. I easily blocked most attacks and hit back in whatever way presented itself.

We danced like this until we were both sweating. When he stepped back, he gave me a deep bow with his right fist cupped in his left hand, held out in front of him. I did the same, signaling the end of the bout. My eyes were wide; my breath was fast.

"What just happened?" I asked.

"You relaxed."

"Come here, girl," Murray called. He was standing in front of a steaming bucket of water. "Take this to yer pallet and wash up. We'll turn our backs."

I looked down at little brown Murray who had cared for me so diligently, fed me from a spoon, and cleaned my most private places after my darkest moments.

"Why would you do that? You know what I look like. So does Lou."

"Yea, well, it be time fer ya to larn some modesty, as they say. Ya aren't a babe now. Ya's a grow'd up woman. I have not a care o'course, being a Broonie. But Lou, now he's a man. Ya need to larn some care."

"Lou knows me inside and out, Murray."

"Thas the truth fer sure, but I be wantin' yer to larn modesty. Time ya be wearin' one o' them shifts ya made too. So yous clean up and put on yer skirts." He had his hands on his hips, and I thought about my mum taking that same tone.

I looked over to Lou's pallet for support, but he was nowhere to be seen. I picked up the bucket, took it to my area, and found soap and a rag. A shift and shirt were all ready for me on my pallet, complete with a soft, woolen shawl. As soon as I removed the breeks, they disappeared. That was Murray's way of pushing me into my young womanhood.

I felt a little self-conscious as I walked over and sat down for our dinner. Murray ignored me, and Lou was not in the cave. We ate without talking, but I began to relax. Murray sat back. His hands were clasped over the round bulb of his stomach, and he had his feet up on a rock.

A tea kettle bubbled over the fire, and the sound of it reminded me of contented evenings around the fire in my own croft with my mum. I would never have such contentment. I would be a mercenary for the Slig Maith.

I got up, and I was pouring tea when Lou appeared at the cave opening. "It's time to talk about magic," he announced.

My heart skipped a beat at the thought of finally being let into the secrets of magic.

"It's about time, me thinks." Murray turned his head to glance at me.

I was clean, and I wore a soft, almost white blouse that covered my neck and arms. The brown shift was coarse and straight-cut, reaching to the floor. I tied a thick rope belt around my waist, and I covered my hair with the shawl. It was long enough to wrap around my neck and over my shoulders. If I had a pin, I could secure it. Instead I would just have to keep throwing the ends over my shoulders when they came loose.

I felt different. I felt grown up. *Could a shift actually grow me up in a matter of minutes?* What a strange feeling this was. I felt like I was in charge. I could do anything. I could make decisions and go my own way. I was no longer a little girl, and yet I was more than a powerless woman. The thought sent a surge of force through my body like a bubbling fountain from the earth. It started in my toes and frothed up my legs, into my belly, up my spine, and into my neck and head. It burst out the top of my head and fell back down around me. I gave myself a little shake. That settled things down a bit.

Lou came and stood in front of me. Murray got up and stood just behind him. He had a satisfied smile on his wrinkled Broonie face. His eyes glistened with tears.

Lou bowed deeply. "You will not need magic with men or women. Just looking at you will bewitch them."

"She'll need it to keep the men away, I'll wager," cried Murray.

I looked down at my peasant's clothing. I owned no shoes. My feet were sturdy, rough, and calloused. "You two jest with me, of course. I am not a lady, just a peasant girl in homespun wool. Meant to work, marry, and bear a child or two. If I had my way, I'd be invisible. My future will be short, my deeds will be terrible, and yet I must get them done and as soon as I can. There will be no life for me. This I know and have known."

Lou turned away. He walked to the tea pot and beckoned me to a seat near the fire. Murray was no longer smiling. A concerned frown now wrinkled his brow. He took my hand and led me to the fire. We all sat there, sipping our tea for a moment.

"Actually, Murray," Lou said, staring out into the dim cave, "you are right. Magic is about time and more." He paused and, looking at me, continued, "There are things you need to know about magic. First, in magic, there is no time. That is because this mind can be in more than one place at the same time." Lou continued as if he were talking to himself. "Second, we are not our bodies. Bodies are tools for our minds. But we are also not our minds. That is another lesson."

He paused to take a sip of tea. "Third, imagination is useful for magic, not so much for fighting, as I have told you. The better you are at knowing the senses of your body, the better will be your magic." He swirled the tea around in the cup. "Last, what you learn and what Mr. Broonie knows by instinct, as a magical creature, is how to manipulate the smallest particles. It is the power of the mind; it is manipulating time and space."

I leaned forward, the half-full cup of tea forgotten in my hand. I kept thinking he would say something I could understand, something I could grasp. But so far there was nothing. To me, space was the space between things, and time was day to night, season to season. Only a god could change those things. My enthusiasm was waning. It was impossible. I would have to carry on without magic. It was obviously too difficult for me. I leaned back in my chair, feeling numb and defeated.

Lou ignored me. "Your practice tonight is to focus your mind on something you choose. Anything, just not too big and something not alive at first. Food is okay. By focusing, I mean see, feel, taste, smell, and hear it so clearly in your mind that it becomes perfect in your mind's eye. I want you to create two things, one at a time, with perfect focus. You have the rest of the night to do this, and we will talk in the morning. Do you understand?"

"Yes, Lou," I mumbled.

I was already trying to think of an object to focus on. I got up slowly and walked to my pallet as if I were in a dream. *How could I possibly be so focused?* It was impossible. But it was also exciting. Finally I was learning about magic. *How could I put together the smallest particles? Where did they come from?* I thought I had to have an incantation, a magic wand, or something magical. *Should I think about food? Maybe an apple like the one Lou had conjured the day we met. Or maybe a pair of boots? Or a broach for my scarf?*

I tucked my legs up under me and searched my memory. Something I had never seen before would be easier to focus on than something I had. That way, I could make it all up. Food would need a taste. I could do an apple. It was my favorite food, but how to think about taste?

I settled on a broach. A shiny copper circle came to my mind almost on its own. In the middle was the imprint of an oak leaf etched on its surface. I turned it over, and a long, pointed pin was attached. In my mind, it moved all around. I could see it's every detail, and I verified that it would work nicely as a broach. It fit into the palm of my hand perfectly.

This was easy! What to do with it now? A box appeared in my mind. It was just the right size. I put the pin in the box and set it on a cupboard shelf, somewhere in my mind.

The pictures were coming to me fast. *A horse? Too big. A sword? Maybe. A pie? Too complex. An apple? Too easy. A loaf of bread, warm out of the laird's oven?* I settled on that.

Before I saw it, I smelled it, the sweet, aromatic odor of wheat, not rye, as it cooked. I had experienced that smell a few times in town. The laird often delivered sweet loaves still warm to the kirk on a day when I was with my mum selling herbs. I could smell it on the back of the cart, and one time, I even followed it, with my nose in the air, just to watch as they dropped off the loaves at the kirk. I wasn't the only kid in town there that day.

I remembered the taste of it mostly from the times Murray conjured it. It was sweet and sour, crusty on the outside, soft and light, and steamy moist on the inside. It was more delicious than the rye bread I was used to. The oven door opened in my mind, and I pulled out a plump, brown loaf, hot and steaming in its pan. I could feel the heat on my face as I looked it over, and the smell was like heaven.

I fell asleep, dreaming of wheat bread, and didn't awaken until my raven walked into the cave the next morning. He was pacing and clucking in front of me when I opened my eyes. I had toppled over onto my pallet in the night, and someone had covered me with blankets. I was in my shift, and my scarf was tangled around my neck. The smell and taste of bread was still in my mouth. Murray walked over as I arose. In his hands were a fresh loaf of brown wheat bread and a small, open box with a copper broach, an oak leaf etched upon it.

"You did it!" he whispered.

11

THE SLIG MAITH

It was a warm and clear day in midsummer, and I was at a small pool in the creek that was downstream of the cave. There was a large, flat rock where I could sit and dangle my feet and legs into the pool. Lou and I had just finished a long practice session ending in a bit of a skirmish. I was shocked to think that I was starting to be an opponent for him. A fog in my brain was opening up, and I had more space for attention. I learned that my mind and body could move around easily in that space. The realization gave me comfort. I felt capable and strong.

Could this be peace? No! The voice in my mind shouted. *No peace for you. Don't forget your purpose. You get no peace, no contentment, and no happiness. Ever.*

A single tear squeezed out of my eye. I materialized a small rag and dampened it in the creek. Since that night some months back, when I had magicked the broach and the bread, I had no trouble manifesting small, simple items. I had not advanced to more complex objects yet because of the dependence issue, specifically the dependence of all things. This was a dangerous issue. No one knew the outcome of manipulating particles and creating things that didn't exist before. I would get it, and the magic would come. There was no doubt. I put the cool, damp cloth over my face and lay back on the moss-covered rock. Dangling my feet in the icy pond, I fell asleep.

I awoke to the woofing flow of breath from a horse, and the vague feeling of possible harm resonated up to me from near the pond.

My raven called from a treetop, "What! What!"

All other noise stopped. Slowly I raised the cloth from my eyes and lifted my head. The forest was still. My beating heart was now its beating heart.

On the other side of the pond, a weary knight sat atop his charger and stared at me wide-eyed. His horse munched grass with loud screeching pulls, shredding each mouthful and chewing with greedy chomps.

Because of my training, I moved carefully. My bared legs needed covering, but my shift was bunched up around me, and there was no way to graciously move. My hair hung in long tendrils like the moss hanging down from the trees. I used it to cover me up a bit as I sat up and tried to collect myself. I stood up.

The man, still gaping, asked, "Who might you be?" Wonder rose in his face.

He was not an old man, but the way he sat his horse spoke of extreme tiredness or a wound. His shoulders hunched, and his arms were limp.

"Can you not speak? Perhaps you are deaf?" He yelled the latter words, and I could feel them rattle around the trees and off the water in a cascading tremble.

His horse gave a start but remained in place, testing the air with flaring nostrils. He patted the horse softly. "No, no, all be well, Curly. Don't take offense yet." It settled again to crop grass at the water's edge.

"Who are you, lass? A wood nymph? If so, lucky me. A baobhan sith come to drink me blood? If so, unlucky you. Mayhaps one of the Good People. If so, I'll be collecting my wish, thank you."

All the pieces of my body wanted to flee as I stood up. "I am not a one of those, my lord, just a peasant girl stealing some coolness in summer. You startled me is all. I'll be off now, back to work." I turned to make my escape.

"Hold, girl! I'm wanting to know more of you. Where be your croft? What is your name?"

His horse stamped a foot and blew out a noisy blast of air.

"All is well, Curly, my boy. You too. Stand still, just a minute more."

I liked the way he talked to his horse. It was obvious to me they were friends. But men were not to be trusted. I knew the dangers of being prey to a man's whims. I had to think fast for my life or use my incomplete skill on a knight. Lou said, if I were in a fight, I was to fight to kill. A knight might be missed, if I did succeed. People would wonder and come to look for him. The only people who would miss me were Lou and Murray. More than likely, I would fail in a fight, and they would find me with a blade in my throat.

Before I could do a thing, the knight's eyes rolled back in his head. He slumped to one side and then toppled off Curly in a slow but hard fall to the ground. Curly didn't move, except for his mouth, which crunched lazily on the grass he had just pulled up.

I ran up to where I could cross the stream and down toward the fallen man, not directly to him though. I knew that chargers were trained to protect their riders, so I slowed as I approached him until I stood a few steps in front of one of Curly's big, inquisitive eyes. He continued chewing. I stood still.

He took a few noisy chews and then raised his head and fluttered his ears back and forth for a moment, looking me over. He took a step toward me and reached out with his nose. He briefly touched my stomach, blew out a belch of air, dropped his head, and moved away from the man on the ground. I knew then I could approach.

He was a big man. It took all my strength to roll him to his back. I listened for air from his nose as I held my hand over his heart. There was a beat. I could not hear a breath, but there must be one. My mind was racing. *Run and get Lou? Try to heal this man with my imperfect magic and send him on his way?*

Before I did that, I needed to know what ailed him. It felt very strange to touch him, and peering under his clothes just wasn't right. *What would my mum do? She would definitely find a wound.*

I felt the bones in his neck and checked his skull for puncture. He had wavy brown hair with blond bits intermixed, due to the sun, no doubt. It was long, down below his shoulders. His face and neck were tanned to an orange-brown hue, and he was long of body and face. I found the wound under an old and bloodstained bandage under his shirt. It was an arrow wound in his right shoulder. It was not life endangering as such, but it seemed he had lost a lot of blood. The wound was in danger of going rotten and needed to be cleaned.

It took a moment to gather my thoughts. I grabbed the knife from his belt sheath and cut a gap in his shirt. I decided to listen to Lou's teaching. Magic of major proportions could be dangerous, not necessarily to the mage, but to the future of everyone. Lou taught me that, if I moved something from one place to another, it could upset the balance that had been maintained. I hadn't been totally successful at conjuring, but after the first magic session when I created the broach and the bread, Lou said I was very good.

"Now you need to be very careful," he said.

"Does this include the smallest particles? I thought they were everywhere?" I asked him once.

He told me that the smallest particles were everywhere and everything. We didn't know where we got them when we made magic. Because of that, illusion was sometimes a better option than creating a physical object. An illusion could be put into the mind of another, but *qi* was needed to sustain it. Since it wasn't real, the mage needed to support it.

I didn't think that magicking a bowl with warm water, some soap, and a cloth would make too big of a difference in the world. I undid the man's filthy bandage and washed the wound. It was indeed an angry red, and the small hole reeked of rot. I washed it out as well as I could. Some drawing herbs were what I needed, along with clean bandages. Oats and milk came to mind. I quickly called them forth. Some bramasog was growing in a sunny spot not far away.

I pulled the roots, avoiding the sticky, round burrs as best I could. I cleaned the roots in the stream and chewed them into a pulp. I added that to the oat-and-milk mixture for a poultice that I secured over the wound with strips of cloth from the sleeve of his shirt.

When I was done, the sun was waning. No sound or movement had come from the man lying there in front of me. Every now and then, I could see some movement behind his closed eyelids. He would live. I was sure. With the help of magic, I gathered brush to build a shelter over him. I took some things from his horse, a bag of wine strapped to the saddle along with a small bag of dried meat, and placed them on the ground next to him. I would have unsaddled his horse, but I didn't know how. I knew the animal wouldn't leave his side.

Walking back to the cave, I went slowly. It had been a long time since someone besides Lou and Murray had talked to me. Murray didn't count. He wasn't human. Lou was like a big brother or even my da, if I really thought about it. I hadn't been down to the village for at least three years. I hadn't even seen another soul since my mum was killed. *Who is that man lying back there, and would he have hurt me if he could?*

A patch of creamh plants caught my eye. They still had the crown of small purple flowers on top of a long, green stem. Not only were they a fine herb, able to keep wounds from festering, they were good for the stomach and pungently tasty too. I carefully dug the soil from around each small, white bulb until I had a large handful. The bulb, stock, and flowers too, we would eat for dinner.

Just as I released the last plant I wanted from the earth, a large and broad pair of soft leather boots and green leggings stepped up from nowhere. I had my head down and was sitting on the ground when they appeared. I slowly looked up into the face of a clean-shaven, well-dressed man. I was dwarfed sitting there in front of him. He had an aura of Slig Maith about him, and yet to my feeling sense, he was not.

"Well, well, missy, will ya come with me peaceably, or will I ha' ta throws ya o'r me shoulder?" He had a catlike grin with feral teeth just showing between wet lips.

"How could I come in any way but peacefully?" I asked in a small, helpless voice. "But my lord, where would you be taking me?"

I got up slowly. As I stood in front of him, I noticed he was still a giant, at least four times as broad as I was and very tall.

"I'm the delivery boy to the Good People, and they require an audience wit ya. My, you are a wee thing and purty too. I might just sling ya o'r me shoulder fer the fun of it."

He reached down, grabbed both my wrists, and gave me a tremendous pull. In that moment, when he expected resistance, I went with his pull. He might have been a good fighter in a battle of foot soldiers with a sword or axe, maybe even a good wrestler. But as Lou told me, he didn't know how to fight someone who did not resist his power. He was off balance as I came at him.

I was a whirlwind. With a slight move of my wrists, I broke his hold. And in a flash, the force of spiraling wind released through my fingers as they drove up into his throat, and I crashed my knee into his privates. He fell onto the ground with a strangled gasp. True to my training, I had my bare foot at the crook of his neck for a killing blow when a commanding voice yelled, "Hold!"

I jumped away from the man and readied myself for the next opponent, who probably had a bow trained on me. I didn't have the wits about me to create a weapon, but I did think "shield." The man on the ground moaned and moved, but suddenly his body disappeared. A pile of ash was all that remained. I didn't have time to be shocked. My shield covered me in a shimmering bubble, and I was ready for any attack.

No bow aimed an arrow at me. A tall, young man stepped out from the forest edge. Well built and comely, he was clean shaven, and his black hair was cropped short. He had a sharp but pleasing face, and the sun had browned his skin. But his most appealing feature was the icy blue of his eyes.

They bore into me, daring me not to notice him. He wore green leggings and a belted green tunic. I knew I should give him a curtsy, but on second hand, maybe he should give me a bow. For some reason, I had no patience for the Good People. Their godlike bearing didn't impress me. I let the shield dissipate. The Slig Maith had come to get me.

"Your fighting prowess is most exciting. It works for you as long as your opponent is surprised," he said gaily. "I imagine you have a few more tricks in you?"

I stood very still, as tall and straight as I could. It really wasn't a question. "Why did you send that poor man to get me? He must have known he couldn't leave your realm for this one."

"He knew all right. But the bargain was, if he were to bring you back, we would have let him go. He was counting on delivering you. You would have kilt him. The magic from our realm got him instead. The death you gave would not have been fast." The Slig Maith moved over to a boulder and leaned up against it as if we were neighbors having a chat behind our crofts.

I folded my arms over my chest. "What now?"

"I've come to invite you to our realm for a brief meet with me mum. She requests an audience." He stood up and swept into a formal bow. "She told me to say please." He was grinning from ear to ear, but I didn't think he was mocking me. It was very strange. He was being playful.

"And if I say no?" I asked bluntly.

"Then I am directed to plead and grovel and to give ya cause to know the importance and gravity of such a meet. I am to assure you that no ill will come to you. No time change will happen, and when you return, all will be well."

"If I still say no?" I was peevish. I'd almost killed a man.

"Then I am to tell you we, as in my mother, who you may know by now is queen in our realm, will visit harm to someone you love. I might add that outcome is totally avoidable. She wants to talk to you, not harm you." He leaned back on the boulder, and he was looking at his fingernails.

"Harm someone I love?" I squinted at him. "Who could that possibly—?"

Then suddenly it came to me, Murray or Lou. I had no doubt the queen was powerful enough to wipe out Murray, as well as Lou, even though both had magic of their own. She could capture them, surprise them, or somehow get to them, and I'd never see them again. I felt like growling. I was trapped. I never considered that friendship and love could be used as a weapon against me.

"I'll go."

Defeated, my body wanted to crumble. It felt bad to lose. But Lou had told me to invest in loss, learn from it, take it to heart, make the best of it, and, in that way, never step aside. I now realized that Murray and Lou meant more to me than my own self. There was danger in that.

"Right," he said as he stood up. "Follow me then."

"We are goin' right now? May I not ready myself? At least tell Murray I'll be gone?"

"Now's as good a time as then." His icy eyes twinkled. This was just a game to him. "We'll have ya back afore dark."

That remained to be seen since dark was very close. He turned to go into the woods, and I followed. I felt the magic in the air shift before I saw it. It was like a thin veil of prickling, sparkling dust that shimmered and waved in the air. He walked through, and without hesitating, I joined him on the other side.

I followed closely on his heels, not sure of where I was. The forest wasn't different from where I had been, but the feel of it was different. The air was damp with promise, like water bringing flowers in the spring. We had stepped into a spring time of potential. I could feel the magic of the place just waiting for the touch of a mage. The magic seemed to grow on me, as if it could sense that I could use it. It wanted to be used. It felt playful and alluring, like an adoring puppy jumping at my heels. I pushed it away. My minor skills could not match the Slig Maith in their realm.

It was a short walk to the edge of the forest. When we walked out from the trees, we stood on a high hill overlooking an open land. It was not covered in heather, as my Highlands would have been, but covered in green grasses about ankle high. I saw a sea of green as far as the eye could see. The blue sky came down to meet it at the horizon. It was not a flat horizon but mounded in soft hills. Two horses grazed on the next hill over.

When they saw us, they lifted their heads and ran toward us. It thrilled me to watch them canter gracefully with their heads arched and manes and tails flowing. One was white; the other was black. Watching the black horse was like staring down into a dark and deep hole. In that moment, I knew he was for me.

"Ah, the beauties." The prince smiled as he watched them come, as enraptured as I.

"Oh yes! My lord, they are wonderful." I was transfixed as they came closer.

"These are of our finest stock, descendants of the terrible Each Visge. These here eat grass and oats like a regular horse. They may kill upon occasion and are useful in that way. Their canines have become small and not so prominent to the casual observer. They are our friends and partners. No need for bridle or saddle. This black is for yourself. A gift from the Slig Maith."

How could I accept such a gift? How could I refuse it? I wanted that horse with a desire I had never felt before. *What I would be able to do astride that beast!*

The horses trotted right up to us. Without any hesitation, the black came to me. I stood still but couldn't keep from shivering. Pent-up *qi* was bursting from my skin. The black tossed his head. He felt it too. We were meant for each other in a way that gave us instant affinity. He was so huge that I couldn't reach my hand to his back, and his feet were immense, but I wasn't afraid. He knew me; I knew him. He lowered his head to my chest and took a long comforting inhale. We breathed each other in, and then I knew he wanted me to ride him.

"Well, my young one, what say ye to a ride?" The Slig Maith prince looked down at me from the back of his silvery-white animal. Its eyes were blue, and he seemed to be as merry as the young man astride him.

"It is my will, my lord. Yet I'm too small. How can I possibly climb onto that perfect back on this most perfect being?" I felt his wanting for me to ride, but I saw no remedy to my lack of stature, unless I climbed a tree or a very large boulder. I was almost in tears. Never mind I had never been on a horse.

"I think it might be possible for ye to jump," the prince said with a mocking look of intense concentration.

"Lou hasn't taught me to fly yet, sire."

"Oh, don't call me that!" He laughed. "Please know my name. It's Cullan. If you allow me, I will call you by your name, Bernadette."

"Yes, Cullan. I have been known all my life as Bernie. Take your pick."

I felt my horse's hot breath on my face as his nose came close. It felt like love. A picture formed in my head. It was of my great horse friend buckling his four legs to bring his huge body to the ground. And this he did. His back legs bent like he was going to sit on his tail, but his front legs went out in front until he was on his stomach. It didn't take me a moment to reach for the hair on his withers and swing myself onto his back. My shift wasn't wide enough for me to straddle. In a blink of an eye, I caused it to tear apart so my legs could hang. In a second blink, my great black horse was on his feet.

It never crossed my mind to wonder if I could ride a horse. In the moment of his walking, we became a single being. When he sprang into a gallop, I leaned into his neck and felt his mane brushing my face. Closing my eyes, I could be flying. His mane was a cloud whipping by me, and with each gathering of his powerful body, I streaked across the sky. We could reach the sun in any moment. We were flying so fast. He ran in total freedom, and yet our minds were so joined together that I knew his actions and thoughts. He ran because he was in love with life, and it was out of sheer joy that I perched on his back. I had not felt such happiness since I was a wee young girl. My meeting with the queen was forgotten.

When we slowed, Cullan and his white mount were beside us. My black pranced happily, and I felt complete. His name was Ciaran. Cullan looked at me with wondering eyes, and maybe a little fear wrinkled his tanned brow.

"That was riding!" he said, his voice low and brimming with admiration. "When did you have a chance to larn that in ye wee short life?"

"I'm fifteen years, goin' on sixteen now."

How dare he call me a bairn!

"I di' na' mean that you are too young," Cullan said without looking at me. "Tis just that ... Well, Slig Maith have different growth rates."

"What do you mean by that?" I was puzzled. If I had to guess, I'd say he had twenty years, at most.

"I mean ..." he continued looking into the sky as if he preferred not to be talking about this at all. "I mean that, since we live so long, we don't even keep track of years like you do, and I am ... Well, I am much older than ye be."

"How much older?"

"Tis hard to be perfectly accurate, but tis on the measure of eighty or ninety years." He turned to see my reaction.

The shock of it ran right through me like a ripple of wind through a tree. Poor Ciaran came to a sudden stop. "No! I'll never believe that!" It was a strange jest indeed.

"Truth," he said. "And I am very young still. My mum be so old that no one is quite sure how many human years she be. I don't think she knows herself."

There was a long pause as I sat frozen in disbelief, yet Cullan continued, "So when did you have a chance to larn to ride like that in yer fifteen years, missy?"

"I have never been on a horse in my life. This one here, he is my own body, and it is truly a marvelous gift he gives me. His name is Ciaran." I sat tall and erect. My *energia* seemed to flow from him as we continued to walk. I did not care how old Cullan was.

We entered a grove of sparsely growing, tall, white trees whose leaves quaked and shivered with sparkling intensity in the light breeze. They made a sound very much like a soft rain on a thatched roof. We walked with a purpose in a direction I had no idea of. I was in constant connection with Ciaran, my black, and realized I could see with his eyes, feel with his skin, and hear with his ears.

With him, the world in this magic realm was so alive that I could hear the creatures under the ground. Birds high in the sky became points of awareness. Small beings in the trees could bring information. Ciaran was aware of everything for miles away and informed my senses of a Slig Maith here and there in the thickening forest, now increasingly of strange, gnarled old pines. Only through his senses did I know we had entered the village of the Slig Maith queen.

12

THE PRINCE

There was no fanfare for the prince when he returned to the village, if I could call it a village. The Good People did not build square buildings like we did. Nor did they build round ones. It seemed that some of them lived in burrows among the roots of the oldest trees, the variety of which I had never seen before. Their most striking feature was their width. If twenty of me held hands in a ring around one of them, I still didn't think we would touch. The roots started high up on the trunk, fanning out like walls and crawling along the earth, more like legs and feet, creating mazes that had pathways around the giant living structures.

There was a thoroughfare of sorts that the horses meandered down, swinging heads and tails in comfortable companionship. Very few people were about. Once, I saw someone out in the woods stop and stare. She had a basket and disappeared behind a wall of tree root as we rode by.

The horses stopped, and Cullan slid off the white. I was considering a graceful dismount but wasn't quite sure how to do it. Ciaran was unconcerned but stood still. I swung my leg over so I was sitting sideways, preparing to slide down, when Cullan appeared at Ciaran's side and reached up. With his hands, he grasped my waist and lowered me slowly to the ground. I had a brief moment of bafflement. Our eyes met midway down, and what I saw there scared me. It was desire.

I knew the stories of young women disappearing because they had caught the eye of a Slig Maith man. It happened to young men too. Slig Maith women were beautiful and powerful. Young men could not resist them. I was not afraid that I could not resist Cullan. *But what kind of power could he wield over me?* I did not want to stay in this realm.

"You intrigue me, Bernie."

He stepped back as he released me. He continued to look into my face, as if looking for something he might recognize. I backed into Ciaran's shoulder, where I seemed to fit as if he put an arm around me, safe and secure.

"Sometimes," he continued, "you are as confident as a Highland cat, and other times you seem as a mouse, about to be caught. What am I to do about you? I fear I am becoming ... attached. No, that tis not it. Let me be honest. I think I would like to know you."

Know me? Should I be relieved? I wasn't sure what kind of "knowing" he meant. Men and women did not "know" each other in my realm. First, they got married, as far as I understood. I was not ready for that kind of knowing. In fact, I had far too much to do before that. My body said "Yes!" but my mind said "No!" I was in the Slig Maith realm, and I let the Highland cat come out.

"I have no time for knowin' you, Prince," I told him as I left the comfort of Ciaran's shoulder. "I need to get back to my home before dark. Where is the queen?"

"You need to clean up before you see my mother," he said with some hesitation, but his gaze never left me. A slow smile grew on his face. "Follow me."

He led me through a rooty maze to a huge giant of a tree. The roots formed a kind of stairway along the trunk. What a strange feeling to be taking step after step up the giant until we reached an open space, like a platform among the leaves. The branches were so tightly woven around it that they created a small room, and at the other end was a short walkway that opened into a rounded, domed space with furnishings: a bed, desk, and chair. In one corner was a large tub full of steaming water. Soap and a small cloth were lying on a low table nearby.

"This be your resting room. Use the tub to refresh yourself. I advise total immersion. It is comfortable and relaxing. Fresh clothing will be brought to you. I will go prepare my mother."

He gave me a quick smile but didn't really look at me, and he backed out of the room, turning to flee as he got to the outer platform.

I didn't waste much time pulling off my shredded shift. I had never had a hot pool of water to jump into. I forgot all of my cares as I settled into the tub and relaxed my bones. I could still feel Ciaran not far away. Someone had brought him a bucket of oats, and he seemed content yet alert. I was not alert. My eyes were closed. I held my breath and sunk fully under the water, feeling its heat cover me in steamy relaxation. *Is this how the Slig Maith lived, like kings and queens in their tree houses high in the air?*

After long minutes, I felt limp and tired. It was time to get out or stay in, fall asleep, and drown.

A woman, carrying a neatly folded pile of cloth, walked in. "Maybe ya hav' na' worn this kind o' clothing afore, deary?" She set them on the bed and held each piece up. "This 'ere ones leggings. Keep ya warm, they will. And better for horse riding. This 'ere is yer tunic, split on the sides, ya see, but long, down to ya's knees. A regular leather belt to tie it to ya. This 'ere is a nice and soft sweater to wear o'r the tunic, made of goat's wool it is, and warm. It'll even shed off water on those damp days. But fer rain peltin' down, a cape, this 'un made of pressed plants for wind and water barrier."

She looked over each item she had laid out on the bed and turned back to me as I hunkered down in the still hot tub. "Do ya need help dressin', missy? Or anythin' at all, just call out Flur, and I'll come to help ya." She gave a little bow and backed out of the room, disappearing at the outer platform as she went down the steps.

When I was dry, I picked up the leggings, a dark forest green. I had never worn leggings. I had never seen a women wear leggings at all. They were very comfortable, wrapping around me and holding on. This was a wealthy man's garment in my world, but I liked the feel of the soft, closely fitting material. There was a short undershirt and then the tunic. It slipped over just like my shift and was about the same color, only lighter brown. Lastly the belt, its clasp in the shape of an oak leaf, reminded me of the broach I had magicked so long ago.

I studied the tight weave in the cloth. The shape of the tunic's sleeve was tighter at the shoulder and upper arm and then gradually widened down to hang over the wrist. I thought the effect was to make one's hands look small and dainty and to allow us to hide them in the billowing sleeves. Or maybe a pocket was sewn inside for dainties like flowers, notes, or small gifts. I looked in one of the sleeves but saw nothing. I was peering into the sleeve when Flur came back in. I dropped it, feeling a bit shy.

"Lookin' for pockets?" she asked with a smile. "It's not a bad idea. Mayhaps you should try one in there. Nothing too big though." Then she held out the boots. I must have looked puzzled. "Never worn boots afore?"

"No," I answered. "Not sure I want to."

"These are special, missy. You'll never want 'em off once you get a feel for 'em. They'er verra soft. Like a pair o' leggin's fer yer feet. And the Slig Maith make 'em fer both yer feet. So's there be a right one and a left one. Not just straight like in your realm. Give 'em a try. If you don' like 'em, I'll eat 'em. Thas how sure I am yer gonna wear 'em."

I sat on the bed, even though I would rather have been lying on it asleep right then. I put the boots on. They were just a piece of leather. The bottom was thicker and stiffer, and the top was soft and pliable. They had hooks that closed them up around your ankles.

"These here are treated for water protection too. Ya knows how leather gets all slimy when it be wet. Walk around. You'll like 'em."

It was strange not to feel the floor, but the boots were soft. They would protect me from sharp rocks and sticks and keep me warm. I decided to give them a try. I could always take them off.

A soft bell chimed, and Flur said, "That be the signal they be wantin' you. Go ahead down the steps. Cullan be waitin' down below."

"Thank you, Flur." I gave her a quick curtsy.

"Don' be doin' that in public." She laughed. "I be the slave help and don' get no thank yous." She paused when she saw the confused look on my face. "That be okay. I am treated fine in all ways. As long as I know me place. Now you run afore Cullan wonders!"

I stared at Flur, a slave. We had slaves in my realm, but I had never met a one. Only the very rich had them, even though the rich could afford to pay for their help. Flur looked healthy and not mistreated at all.

She boldly looked me in the eye. "Be off with ya now, me lass, afore

Cullan comes up 'ere and finds us gabbin'!" She had a twinkle in her eye and a laugh in her voice.

I could feel Cullan watching me as I came down the steps spiraling down the tree. As soon as I approached him, he turned his face to gaze in another direction. I didn't think I was that bad a sight. *Or maybe I was too good a sight?* There was some inner turmoil I felt within him. *Did he hate me now?* I could not discern.

Ciaran broke the spell with a whinny, trotting up to me. He almost pushed Cullan out of the way. He lowered his head, and I flung my arms around him. Being apart would never be easy. For now, I held him, and he held me with his mind until Cullan gave a little cough.

"Excuse me." The laughter was back in his voice. "I can see ye both have been apart so long you need some time alone, but the queen herself is waitin' on ye. Be quick and let's be off. We can walk, Ciaran. No need for riding."

Ciaran opened his left eye and looked at the prince. Then he slowly raised his head out of my arms. He muzzled my forehead with soft lips and backed up a couple steps. I glared at the prince. *Such a frivolous man. Couldn't he feel the deep need Ciaran and I had for each other?*

"This way," he said, ignoring me. But he stopped suddenly, a grin affixed on his lips. "I can see ya little caring for your own looks, me lass, but my mum may not find it charming."

I stopped in my tracks. I looked down at myself, spread my arms, and looked all over my front, down to my toes. "What?" I asked in a whiny voice. Flur hadn't said I'd dressed wrong. "I cannot see anything amiss."

"'Ave ya looked at your head since leaving the bath?" He turned to look at me. The grin was still firmly affixed.

I reached up with one hand to feel my head. It seemed fairly dry.

But now I remembered I had forgotten to brush my hair. I picked up a few coils that straggled down my shoulder. They stuck together in long ropes as wide as my finger.

"I am used to covering my head with a shawl, but one was not available when I left the bath. Nor was I reminded to comb it." Thinking that Flur might get in trouble, I said, "I did not see a comb."

"Ah well," he said thoughtfully. "I didna' think of either of those implements. Flur should have helped me. Never mind. Can you fix it with magic?"

I produced a comb and began to release the snarls and nests of entwined hair. It was going to take some time.

"Never mind!" He laughed. "Will you let me untangle it from here? It won't hurt."

"You mean with your magic?"

"Yea! It be mine!" He laughed. "But it is powers granted to me by this great and powerful forest, a force to be reckoned with fer sure, but safe for you. I can't use it unless you permit me. And in this case, it would be in your own best interest. My mum hates it when one hair is out of place."

I remembered the first and last time I had met the queen. I was sick and dirty. She thought she had the better of me then. Now she thinks I would be a weapon she could wield. I doubted she would care about my hair, but I could see the prince only wanted to help. I looked into his ice-blue eyes and saw there not only his desire but also his uncertainty. He was a young man. My heart softened toward him, and yet I knew I would need my wits with his mum.

"All right," I said. "Just once, go ahead and fix it."

I felt something brush into me like a wind carrying sand, little prickles touching my skin.

"Done," he said with a frown and pierced eyes. "That wasn't easy, but you are ready to meet her now."

I looked at my shoulder and down to the ends of my hair. It trailed down below my waist in wavy strands. All signs of tangles were gone. I ran my fingers through it a couple times. I had never used magic to comb out my hair. I would from now on.

The prince stepped very close to me. I was forced to look up to see his face. Merry eyes in a brown face gazed down at me. Being so close made me feel a little tense. My urge was to step back, but I didn't. Before today, I had never been touched by a man, except Lou when we sparred.

Cullan brought up one hand, and between his fingers was a lovely green satin ribbon. "If you would like to tie your tresses with this ribbon, it is yours."

"Yes, thank you," I whispered. I stepped back, pulled my hair into a tail, and deftly knotted the ribbon around it.

The prince just stared for a moment, and then nodding his head, he turned and started walking. It didn't seem like he desired to kill me after all.

13

BERNADETTE AND THE QUEEN

It wasn't far to the queen's palace, if one could call it that. It was in an immense tree at the end of the thoroughfare. The prince walked quickly with catlike grace. He was long and lean, comfortable in his body. I felt like a child scrambling to keep up behind him. We entered the tree from the foot of the monstrous thing, where an arching doorway between the roots opened down into a dark stairwell. We walked down, and dim lights began to glow, as if our movement caused them to light. A fresh, cool smell came to my nostrils, like the fertile soil of a planted garden, and I could hear some music being plucked in a delicate melody.

The prince lightly skipped down the steps like he had been here many times. He must have used these steps as a very small boy. I followed closely behind, and soon we came out into a large room. Firelight from brands burning on the walls flickered and flared as we walked across the almost empty hall. The musician plucked his instrument in a corner and didn't seem to notice us passing. When we came upon a closed door, the prince rapped his knuckles on it once. It opened from the inside, and we walked in.

The room was lit by a raging fire in a fireplace that took up most of the opposite wall. Shadows flickered and jumped around us. There were no windows. Tapestries lined the walls and floor, but it was too dark and shadowy to see their patterns. The flickering of the blaze made it seem like there was movement where there wasn't, and it put me on guard. I could feel from the lift of his head that the prince himself was alert.

Three chairs were placed near the fireplace. Each one would have seated four of me. They were covered in fabric or leather and plump with stuffing. I had never seen such places to sit.

"Welcome to my home, Bernadette." The queen stood behind one of the chairs.

She was in a gown that matched her hair, a robin's breast orange. The sleeves and neckline were lined in gold. Though I had never seen gold, from the way it shined and sparkled in the wavering light, I knew it was real gold. Diamond earrings glistened, and under the well-placed strands of hair on her forehead, a gold crown shown. She seemed to be trying to befriend me. But I was expecting her tricks, and her words only irritated me.

"My queen," I said in a strained voice.

She laughed a tinkling waterfall sound, and as I felt so many years before, the niggling feeling of enchantment floated around me. She hadn't learned her lesson. I couldn't help it. I grabbed the delicate tendrils she tried to wrap around me with my mind, rolled them into a ball, and threw it into the fire.

"You required a meeting, madam?" I said casually. Any fear of her I might have was dissipating, replaced by a growing impatience. "I did not choose to come here. I was threatened."

She frowned, just a flash of her face. I could see the danger in those piercing green eyes. They turned black for a moment, and her hands started going to fists, but the prince broke in.

"Mother, Bernadette has come to hear your words, not to feel your magic. Shall we sit? I'll call for tea."

"Yes, my son," she said lightly, breaking the tension.

"None for me thank you." I was being careful. It was well known that food and drink with the Good People was dangerous. It could mean being stuck there for years and it seemed only a day.

"Bernie, I told you. You don't have to worry. You'll be back before dark." He looked at me with squinted brows as if I were too young to understand. I was getting tired of being the wee child.

"So you have said." I looked from him to his mother. "But your mum seems to want to turn me with her power. And therefore how can I trust?" I gave her a glare, but she only smiled back, grinning at the child I was, as she spoke to her son.

"Bernie, is it? That's very familiar, son. Yes, please get us tea. Three cups. I will explain to Bernadette."

The prince went out, leaving me.

"Bernadette," she began, "I will be honest with you. You are immune to most of our little magicks. And sometimes special people don't suffer them. Why? I don't know, but I have my suspicions."

She opened her hand and offered me the chair in front of hers. We sat and faced each other with the blazing fire to the side. There was a third chair closer to hers and facing me, for the prince, no doubt.

I would have liked to know what her suspicions might be, but the prince entered and set a tea service on a small table between him and the queen and poured a cup with milk for her and one for me with a spoonful of honey. When we all had our cups, I gave up. The smell of the brewed tea was enticing. I took a sip and relaxed into the puffy chair, the sweetness of honey and chamomile like a balm to my fraying nerves.

"It is good to see you relax." The prince held the cup up to his face and took a deep breath. His eyes closed, and he smiled.

The queen looked from him to me and back. Her face softened briefly. It made her look more like an appraising mother than the dangerous queen she was.

"Yes," she said and took a sip. "You are looking quite like a Slig Maith, my dear, except for the height. Nothing a little illusion charm couldn't take care of. But let's get to business, shall we?

"I called you here to discuss your progress on your path. I hear from my son that in hand-to-hand combat you have some skill. It may be useful. But it is magic that will be the more important tool. I see that you have some minor skill. I think our teacher, Liu Shen, has been slow in his duty."

"Our teacher?" I stiffened in my padded chair, almost spilling the tea. I never thought Lou was a Slig Maith servant. I thought he was a friend to Murray.

"Yes, he is friend to the Slig Maith and knowledgeable in all magic matters. He is also human and therefore a better teacher than a magical being. He had to learn magic directly, unlike Murray, who comes by it naturally. Murray was to train you in language, reading, and writing, which I dare say he has done. Our problem is with Liu."

"Problem?" I searched my mind and could think of nothing that could possibly be a problem. Lou was friend, teacher, and, even more than that, a father.

The queen sipped her tea, watching me over the cup. "The problem is that he has grown quite fond of you," she said, as if it were common knowledge.

The prince shifted in his seat. Obviously this was news to him. I was not surprised. I had fondness for Lou too. But it was not in partnership that my love arose. I doubted that was his form of love either.

"I don't know about the Good People, but we of the other realm have several forms of love. I feel love for Lou, Liu," I corrected. "Tis love for a father or a mentor. I am sure that is Liu's love too, a father to a child or a master to a student."

"It really doesn't matter what kind of love it is. The problem being that he is slow in training you to the grander aspects of magic. I want you ready to perform your duties when the time comes. You remember our bargain?"

"Of course. I have been studying diligently," I answered, but I had wondered about that myself. It seemed that, while slowly teaching me, Lou had warned me. Outcomes of big magic could have effects for many lifetimes, he said. One must be very careful. I thought he just wanted that to sink in.

She saw the understanding on my face. "I see that this is not a new thought for you. Liu is worried for your happiness and doesn't want to teach you to fulfill your destiny because you may suffer." Then with mocking pity in her voice, she said, "What he doesn't know is all the pain you have suffered and suffer now, my dear. Your happiness will only come when you complete your revenge, of course, and satisfy the bargain you have made with us."

She was looking right at me with wide, mesmerizing eyes. I believed her. It was what I had been telling myself forever. I didn't believe in happiness, and I planned to die young. That was what bothered Lou. I suddenly understood.

"What are we to do?" she exclaimed. Her concern was so false that it was almost funny.

I looked at her worried face, but she was laughing behind the mask. She had a plan. She turned to her son, feigning concern. The guise of worry curved her mouth down into a fake frown. I felt more like a wee bairn than ever.

"We want to invite you to stay here and make faster progress with us," he said, his eagerness showing in the lean of his body. "You have the early training in magic. You can learn the rest easily from us."

The prince's face was open with hope for an instant, but not fast enough to evade the notice of the queen. He felt her surprise and curiosity as she stared at him with a wondering gaze. As he rearranged his features into a calm, distracted mask, he turned to drain the teapot into his cup.

Then he lifted the pot, first to his mum and then to myself, with a questioning look. "More tea?"

I felt his hope too. We had known each other for less than a day, and yet I felt a sense of wanting to be with him. It was more than that. It was not just my mind wanting to be near him; I felt this need in my whole body. I could not let my guard down. His mother could see through him. I must not give her any fuel.

"No, thank you." I turned to the queen. "If Lou, I mean Liu, has the knowledge to complete my training, I will go to my own, as I told you once before. I will be more diligent in my studies and demanding in my lessons with him. My revenge I will use as practice sessions for fulfilling my debt to you. If I am not sufficiently trained and have completed my own mission, I will come to you for more training, provided you do nothing to hurt Liu or Murray but let them live out their lives as they will."

"I always thought Liu would be an asset if he could be convinced to our cause. Now you will be his conviction."

She looked at her son, who was not hiding his disappointment very well.

I could almost hear her mind as she thought up new ways of controlling him, with myself as the bait, no doubt.

"There may be one other enticement for you to consider." She turned back to me. "Your friend, our Black, you have named him Ciaran." She paused to check her teacup. "He is for your use when you are here, but he is for only limited use in your realm. If you need some transport to complete your revenge, you may entreat his aid. But that is all until you see fit to honor your promise to us. He will be waiting for that day, my child."

This was like a blow, a punch to my stomach. I thought he was mine. I tried to remain calm. I knew there was no arguing from the look on her face. She was ready for a tantrum from the bairn I was. I wasn't going to give it to her.

The queen continued, "I can't understand how you can refuse our hospitality. You could live like a queen here, but I see that love is strong for your friends. This, you also know, is a dangerous thing, and I would encourage you to be careful in the future."

She passed a glance to Cullan. "You must choose your friends wisely. Maybe none is the better counsel?" She stood up. Her son stood as well, so I followed. "Cullan will show you back to your woods. Until we meet again." She tipped her head.

I bowed, and she turned and walked out of the room by another door. She had given me fair warning. The only person I needed to fear for the safety of friends was she.

The prince seemed in deep thought. He must have been surprised at my forward behavior with the queen. I was sure he could not believe I would tell her no. I tried to get his attention. Maybe he would tell me his thoughts, but without saying a word, he turned to leave the room, and we retraced our steps out of the giant tree palace.

"Can you call Ciaran to your side?" he said as soon as we stood outside.

Since I knew at all times where Ciaran was and he knew of me, he was already on the way. I didn't have to say a thing. We could hear his hooves thudding on the soft forest ground. As soon as he came into view, he gave a loud whinny. Right behind him was Cullan's white.

"You two have an uncommon connection, and that's fer sure." The prince scratched his chin. "I hope he will be able to endure your absence while you finish yer training." I sensed there was something more he wanted to say but did not.

I hadn't thought about Ciaran missing me. I wondered about myself. *How could I be parted now that I had found him?*

"The queen said I could use him if I needed him. Just that we couldn't stay in my realm until our bargain had been commenced."

I couldn't take my eyes off him as he trotted up, threatening to bowl me over until the last moment when he stopped in front of me, pushing gently against my chest and face with his soft, warm nose. He smelled like spring grass and horse.

"That she did, Bernie. Ye best get along with yer training," he said, smiling. "Let me help ye to mount. Stand facing his left side and bend yer left leg. I'm going to hold yer ankle, like this. When you feel me pick it up, ye take the momentum to fling your right leg o'r his back. Got it?"

It worked. It was a little like a jump, only assisted. The prince heaved only slightly. I was sure it was nothing to him, and I could use the power of his throw to glide onto Ciaran's back. Ciaran tossed his head up and down in approval.

"Someday you will use magic."

"Either that or I must practice vaulting or use a large rock or low tree limb as an aid?" I was only partially kidding.

On the back of this magical animal, I felt powerful and tall. There was nothing I couldn't do. With the senses that we shared, I had no doubt we would be formidable in any situation. The prince sprang to the back of his white, and we walked out of the Slig Maith village.

We ambled along in silence for awhile. I knew what the woods were to my mount. He felt safe and unconcerned. He communicated to the white as we walked. They seemed to be close friends. Between the two of them, nothing could escape our attention. The prince seemed quiet, pensive. Something was bothering him.

"I need to tell you about the Slig Maith," he finally offered.

We were out of the trees and crossing the grassy hills.

"That would be good." I wanted to hear him speak. I would be happy to hear anything, but this was a good topic. When some moments went by in silence, I said, "Go on then. What say you?"

I could feel him gathering his thoughts. "We have a two-court system in our government. The courts exist to offer advice to the queen. The people of the courts are men and women of the eldest of our race, those of us who have survived sometimes hundreds of years. We are a long-lived people. We live long, but our numbers grow very slowly."

"You have women on your courts?"

"Yes, of course. Each individual has a unique perspective based on the experiences of his life. Each has developed judgments and beliefs based on those experiences. We deem these elders learned and educated and therefore use them in counsel to the queen.

"They are called the Seeley Courts, made up of the Seeley Council and the Unseeley Council. They best represent our history and knowledge, and while the queen makes the decisions, they point her to the best choices. One of the courts does not have a favorable view of our cousins, the humans of your realm. We have record of a time when your race was a lowly animal, living in holes and wearing skins. You had rudimentary skills and were easily frightened and manipulated. Your numbers were few, and we had little reason to encounter you. You served us no purpose at all. You did advance, obviously, and became more self-aware. As you did so, you chose us as your gods and worshipped us with elaborate ritual. You saw your connection to the land, and you worshipped us to get our help.

"Those were golden years for us. We could walk on the land without a care. We could mingle with you and we thrived in your love. The land thrived, the forests grew, and the magic in them was healthy and strong. Your kind chose not to be magical; they easily lost interest in the help we could bring and sometimes took offense at the payments we took. You were soon finding new gods to help you, rich gods from other places. You began to fear us, your local gods, and turned to gods that didn't even exist here.

"Soon these gods scared you too. But your fear of them was stronger than your fear of us. You grew up with us. We were familiar, and you had ways to avoid us. These new gods were different. They were fierce and controlling. Their human representatives wielded a power in your realm much stronger than ours was. Fear of pain and suffering were their tools. Even after death!"

"Hell," I blurted out.

"Yes," he said. "I believe that's what it's called. Can you imagine being afraid of something after death? I guess that life under these new gods is so miserable that one can only hope it will get better after death!" He laughed. "Too bad we didn't think of this!"

"But," I stammered. "Why do the Good People have any care for the human condition? If they want to, they can do what they will. Why bother when your realm is so beautiful and full of life?"

"Ah, and this is where the understandin' becomes complicated." He paused for awhile. It seemed he was having trouble knowing how to continue. "The Slig Maith and the human realms are connected. We have a saying, 'as above so below.' What happens in your realm impacts ours. When we lost your love, we lost part of ourselves. Your fear affects your realm in ways you would never know. The cutting of woods with no care for the order of it weakens our forest; your gluttony and your need to dirty whatever you touch reaches to us. And even after this latest die-off, the Black Plague, your population quickly rights itself and increases with such amazing capacity that there is no controllin' it.

"We can no longer bear your realm. As the keepers of nature in both realms, we can no longer watch as you destroy your nest, and our power to protect it fails us. We have retreated, but some of us are not happy about it. A few in our society believe that humans are no better than livestock, to be used or to be slaughtered. This is not a new thought, but it has become increasingly popular. It is now a belief shared by the queen and some in the Seeley Council."

My mind was swirling with all this information. I had never realized that humans were destroying the very land they lived on. Before I could collect my thoughts, he went on. "The two councils have two different approaches to our dilemma. My mother is with the Unseely Council. She believes we must destroy humankind right away in order to protect what we have and what we are as keepers of the natural order. That is what all the murderin' creatures are all about. The problem is your kind has over whelmed them. There are too few to do the job. She feels that, when we do remove humans, we will reign over both realms with no interference from those angry gods that the humans use to explain their destructive ambitions."

He looked over at me. He wondered what my response would be, but I had no tongue. My mind was full of confused thoughts, and I could bring nothing to the fore. We rode for awhile in silence.

"The Seeley Council recommends acceptance. They believe it is the human's destiny to rule their realm and make their own choices. Our demise will be slow, as will theirs. We may yet prevail through education. We are not above infiltrating human life and causing them to see their violence to nature, without annihilation of the species. Slig Maith, after all, rarely die. We can watch and wait and then make humans see their greed. We don't need to enslave them or kill them all."

Finally I found my voice. "This is news I can't relate to. I must consider it. As you say, total destruction will take a long time if left to our own devices. I can't even imagine what that would look like and why I should worry. I have no love for my fellows. I don't wish them ill for sure, but the caring of them is beyond my strength. Killing them all, now that would be near impossible and unimaginable to me. But I have no doubts your mum has a plan."

We were entering the forest so much like my own, and the horses stopped.

"This is the end of our ride," Cullan said with some disappointment. He slumped a little on his horse's back. "I had wanted to speak of other things, but now I fear my moment is lost. This story I have told is for your own protection."

He slid off his white mount and came over to my black. I towered over him as he looked up at me. He seemed sad. I didn't know what to say. I swung my leg over and slid down as he caught me in his arms. It was a little too close. He pressed me into his chest, and his lips brushed my hair as he lowered me to the ground. I did not struggle.

Ciaran stamped and blew out air. He woke me up as I realized Cullan and I had been gazing into each other's eyes—he with a mixture of concern and desire and me with confusion and longing. *What was I longing for? What was this strange feeling?* My body tingled from the inside out. My young heart, beating out of my chest, wanted so badly to open up, to encompass Cullan, to be filled with him. My mind felt it as danger.

And no sooner did my heart open was it slammed shut. There was no happiness or love for me. My mum was the last victim of that. The queen had warned me. I knew my life was for other things. I must be hard and unrelenting in my revenge.

Cullan felt my withdrawal. From his look and his sudden stepping back, I could see his defeat, but it was only momentary. He grabbed my shoulders in his hands and held me at arm's length.

"I know what mother said, Bernadette, but you have bewitched me. There is nothing you can do about it. And nothing I have more of than time. I will wait. Know that I will be ready to help you whenever you call. Know that I will be watching and wanting you. Please don't ignore me. I will not go away."

"Right now, I don't want you to go away. But I am afraid for you. My loves are all at risk. It is better not to tempt trouble, as your mother said. I shall have no friends for their own safety. She will use me against you!" I blurted out.

And you against me.

He let me go and took a step back. Gazing out into the woods, he seemed to be at a loss. His mother's threat was clear to me.

"Yes, go now. I won't keep you. The path is clear. You can make the crossing where you will. But know that I will be back to find you."

I turned to give Ciaran a farewell. *Was that a tear I saw dropping from his eye?* I held his great head and felt our connection growing.

"Until we meet again," I said. "My love," I added in a choked whisper.

I needed him more than anything, but I couldn't let that show.

14

LOST

The veil between the realms was very close, and I passed through it to my own familiar woods without looking back. I walked by the pile of ash that had once been a man. All he wanted was to free himself from the Slig Maith. If I were trapped in their realm, I would try to escape too. The creamh bulbs and stocks that I had picked lay scattered around. I thought about picking them up and taking them for dinner, but I didn't want to slow down. Here I was, with the sun continuing to sink, the woods darkening, and my raven calling as he flew above me. Cullan had kept his promise. I would be home by dark.

I could not get the prince out of my head. He was a comely man, so many years older than I was, but still a child to his mum. Just the thought of him set my skin to tingling in a most pleasant way. I knew that there would be nothing come of it, his feelings or mine. He was a prince. *I am ... What am I?*

I was only a person who lived in a cave with a Broonie and a mage from some faraway place. I'd seen Ming on a map that Lou drew on the floor of the cave. I had no notion that the world was that big or that full of people. Lou had been to many places that I didn't have any idea of. Was the realm of the Slig Maith also that big? Maybe it was only the Scottish and British land they were tied to. I would have to ask Lou.

Murray was standing with his thin arms crossed over his chest at the mouth of the cave as I ran up. "Where 'ave ya been, girlie? Ya 'ave a look and feel of Slig Maith all o'er ya. Sumthin's happened." He waved me in with a sweep of a hand.

It wasn't me that he was talking about. I followed him in and felt the wrongness in the cave immediately. Something had happened.

"Ye be comin' 'ome a wee late and wit the smell o' magic all o'er ye, and while ye were gone, we lost Lou," Murray whined in a high nasal voice.

"What?" I tried to remain calm, but my day had been long on surprises.

This news was the last straw. My hands clenched into fists, and I ran over to Lou's corner of the cave. There was nothing there. I stood there and looked all around, willing my personal light into brightness. There was nothing of Lou's left. Even his smell was gone. Nothing remained. I tried to feel his energy as I stood there unbelieving. *Is he dead? How could he leave me now? I was not done with my training. I must find him!*

I ran outside. A brilliant sunset lit the sky in orange and pinks between the treetops, but I didn't care. I tried to feel for Lou's *energia* and *qi*. I searched around the floor of the woods. Maybe he left a trail I could follow. Perhaps the queen called to him. She must know something. Maybe he would be back soon. He had left before for short times, but he had never left and taken everything he had. It was like he had never been there.

Murray came out and put a soft touch of one knobby hand to my arm. "He left ya somethin'," he said, holding out his hand. "It's a talisman o' some sort."

In his hand was a flat, round pebble, and scratched on the surface was something like two fish swimming around each other. They were so close as to be connected in the center. Their bodies formed a perfect circle. One was white with a black dot for an eye; the other was black with a white dot. A leather strip pierced a hole that was drilled on the edge of the stone. It fit around my neck and lay between my breasts in the heart space of my chest.

"I found it on yer pallet," Murray said. "Come in now. We'll ha' tea." He turned, his shoulders more slumped than usual. "Ye needs food. I can tell."

Eating was the last thing I was thinking about, but I managed a few morsels of mushroom and some bread.

"Tell me wot today was fer, ya lass. Something momentous, I'm sure." Murray looked me in the eye. His brows were knitted together in worry and curiosity.

The little fire cracked and popped, throwing shadows across the cave walls. The empty space left by Lou, my teacher for almost three years, was overwhelming. I put my face in my hands and rubbed violently. Maybe this was a dream. When I opened my eyes, Lou would be sitting across the fire, leaning in to hear me.

He wasn't. I rested my elbows on my knees and stared into the fire. I had forgotten I was still dressed in leggings and tunic, with the soft leather boots on my feet.

"From the look o' ye, ya been wit the Good People. What ha' ya to say?" Poor Murray was needing assurance that I was well.

I could hardly speak. "Ye are right." I stood up. "I saw the queen in her own abode. Did she take Lou away? I will kill her." I began to pace in front of the fire. I forgot Murray was there. I was seething.

"An' why would ya think such a thing, dearie? Wot did she say to yas?" His eyes followed me as I stomped back and forth. My hands were behind my back.

"She said Lou wasn't doing his job. Too slow. He did na' want me to complete my revenge. He was afraid for me." I paused to look Murray in the face.

His eyes widened slightly. "She had the right of it fer sure," he said, looking away. "She's a busy old thing."

"I'm not finished with my training!" I cried. "She can't send Lou away now. I told her I would confront him and be more diligent in my studies."

"Did she tell ye to stay in that realm, that they would finish yer training?" He took a sip of tea.

"That is exactly what she said." I sat back down, facing Murray. Maybe he had a plan. "She used her son to entice me," I added, feeling embarrassed.

I now could see the prince was only for attraction. Of course he was purely acting, like a bard on a stage. He was only playing with me. What could be easier to manipulate than a young girl in love? And what young girl didn't dream of attracting a prince?

I didn't want to admit it. I wanted his attention. The queen and her son almost had me fooled. I was ablaze with anger. It was hard to sit next to the fire. I wanted to leap up and go to the queen and Cullan and hurt them.

"Calm down, missy. Here, drink this cool water." He was standing next to me with a cup.

It was herbed water. I could smell it, something calming for sure. I drank it down. My small world had been torn from me. All my comfort was gone. Without Lou, I was without a base. I wasn't ready for my revenge. I couldn't continue. My life had no place to rest, nothing to hold onto.

"Ye be fine," Murray said as he put his arm around me and patted my shoulder. "Lou told me hisself that ye was ready for revenge. An' I 'ave done my best to make ya the lady you are. It's the doin' of the deeds is all. I was hopin' he'd leave ya strong in yer own power to refuse the lady yer bargain. But that is left to be seen. Think. Wot would Lou do?" He gave my shoulder a little shake.

I buried my face in my hands again. It seemed so much easier than facing the empty hole in the cave and the confusion I found in my heart. *What would Lou do?* The question rumbled around in my brain until I couldn't stand it. I got up like a body rising out of a grave and began cat walking in a circle, back foot weighted and front foot grasping the ground and pulling my body forward. With each step, spiraling earth energy pulled down, and spiraling heaven energy pulled up. Arms at ready, I was aligned and facing an imaginary opponent.

Soon I was feeling fluid. The power flowed into me, around me, and out of me. I felt pathways in my body that I could move with. I began a series of training moves, and my mind cleared. I summoned the elements. I was fire raging through the forest, jumping from bush to bush, sticking and crawling up a tree, exploding outward with overwhelming power. I was lightning, sending shocking jolts of energy in rapid and sustained bursts. I was water, flowing in rhythmic movement, heavy and bold, wearing away at obstacles with patience and knowing. I was air, billowing and cool, light and invisible, a tornado of swirling power, overpowering and lifting the heaviest things, breaking and twisting. I became earth, heavy and expansive, ferocious.

Each move flowed into the next until clarity transitioned into nothing. I wasn't there. Over and over, my body walked the circle, sometimes fast with kicks and dips and other times so slow there was hardly a movement at all.

I didn't know when I stopped. My awareness had long left my body. Somehow I made it over to my pallet. Murray had gone to his sleep long before. I stretched out my mind, searching for Lou. He was nowhere to be found.

When awareness of myself and my body returned, I was sitting on my pallet, knees bent under me. I felt as if I had just slept soundly and all was well. A decision was made, and I knew what I had to do.

"Mornin' to ya, me lass," Murray called from the fire. "Ave a cup o' tea and break yer fast with these wee cakes and some porridge."

I was hungry and strangely elated. My worry was gone. I was ready for my path to unfold, be it good or bad.

"I've got to go, Murray. Tis time I pursued my revenge."

"As I thought," he said. "You know I 'ave to stay 'ere. But I will help ye as much as I can."

"I know. I am counting on you. I will need your help with some magic. And you can finish the touches on the lady you've been trying to make of me."

That brightened his face. "I may need more time than I've got fer that project." He grinned. "But you'll do."

15

FORRESGEM

Two weeks to the day after Lou disappeared, I was a proper lady riding a horse cart as if I were a queen. I did my own illusion, which I was quite proud of, but Murray's was truly magic. I didn't know where he found the small donkey and hay wagon. He assured me he would send it home when we were done. The donkey transformed into an old cart horse, and the wagon was a partially covered driving cart. As long as Murray was with them, the illusion would last.

The cart had two wheels and was open on the driving end. The back was covered in a yellow cloth. It was so uncomfortable that I refused to go back there. I sat next to Murray, who looked like an elderly human. He was still short but rounded and taller than a Broonie. The big surprise was that he had magicked some new clothes for himself. I guessed, since it was an illusion, it was okay.

I now had straight red hair that I wore in a tight bun on the back of my head, under a cover, of course. I put some lines in my face and yellowed and crooked my teeth so I would appear much older than my soon-to-be sixteen years. I had a plain, dark blue outer gown, slightly worn. It was nothing fancy, a higher class than where I was coming from.

Murray had schooled me and schooled me until I was red in the face, and now I spoke like a lady, walked like a lady, and ate like one too. I even added some flesh to my middle so as to be sure to not attract any attention. In all ways, I was a matron.

We had thought of everything, at least the details of my identity. The actual doing of the revenge would have to be a product of the moment. I could not risk being discovered, especially if I wanted to use my innocent matron illusion for more than one killing.

Yes, killing. I had thought about killing, and I been trained to kill, but I could not dwell on the reality of doing such a deed. Spontaneity was one thing; plotting and planning was another. Murray counseled me to be cautious and private. A magical being, he was never afraid, but he had fears for me. I did not plan to be away for a very long time, so we knew we would be back together soon.

I had papers from a bishop in St. Andrews saying I was a scribe and knew numbers and could also teach children. It said I was upstanding and a widow and could be trusted to be chaste. The latter Murray thought I should add because widows sometimes had bad reputations. The problem was that I had no other way to explain why I was travelling alone. It was something that decent women did not do. My basic plan was to get employment in the business of Janet's husband and try to find out where she was.

In this way, I arrived back in Forresgem. It was little changed in the four years I had not seen it. My fear was rising. There were so many people and animals. The street was crowded with humans, horses, and carts, all going every which way at that time of day. There was a strong smell of manure and rotting vegetation, along with the yelling and chafing of too many bodies in a small space.

As we clopped down into the dusty town, I leaned over to Murray. "I have never lived in a town! What am I going to do?"

"I truly don't know, Bernadette, I mean Katherine. Make your business fast." He looked at me from the corner of his eye.

Behind the frozen look of indifference on his unfamiliar face, I sensed his strong urge to flee. "My poor Murray, I am sorry to bring you here. Will you be right?"

"Dona' worry 'bout me, missy!" he squealed. "You 'ave to stay. I'll be back in our 'ome by nightfall. And it is there I'll be stayin'." He flicked the reins lightly. "I think our poor old donkey-horse might be fallin' asleep. It's you I am concerned about. I 'ave no knowing how to git aroun' this town. Ye need a room or a boarding house is me guess."

"Take me to the kirk! I can ask there for accommodation. If this is High Street, it is just … right down there." Of course we could see the tallest building in town. It was still imposing, and as he reined in, I could see the doors were open.

"Kind sir," I said as I climbed down off the cart. My extra weight limited me a little. I had to remember I was aged. At least that was my illusion. People would see what they would. I was hoping it would not be Bernadette MacTigue. I was now Katherine Fergus of Edinburgh. "Please wait for me here. I'll only be a moment."

"Yes, madam," said Murray. He kept his head down between his shoulders, holding the reins loosely out in front of him like any paid driver. The horse stood a bit splayed out and dropped its head almost all the way to the ground.

The kirk hall remained the same as my twelve-year-old self recalled.

I walked right up to the tormented statue and looked in his pain-filled face. "Why me?" he was still asking. Even his godliness couldn't save him.

I now understood his pain. It was the same as my mum's. "Why my mum?" I asked him.

"Why any of us?" he seemed to answer.

I felt a tap on my shoulder. I turned with a gasp to face a priest.

"I didna' mean to skeert ye, lady." A very young man stood behind me. "I toht ye might be enraptured, ya know, and that I shud give ya a tap. We 'ere abouts use his holy name vera often in our devotions. His is a strong invocation for help when we are in need."

He seemed such an ardent young acolyte that I didn't have the heart to reprimand him for touching me in such a manner. His eyes were big and round and his pink cheeks grew red as he realized what he had done.

"My name is Katherine Fergus, recently widowed," I began.

He looked up eagerly, wanting to help me from all the naïve craving in his heart.

"I need lodging in this town. I intend to seek employment. I have papers from the bishop at St. Andrews, if it pleases. But right now, I have a cart for hire and a man waiting. Would you have a recommendation of a room for such as myself?"

"Oh yes, lady. There's rooms for hire not so far from 'ere. Unfortunately, they be above the eatery, right there on High Street. I am sure you will find employment quickly and be able to move accommodation. This be only short term. It be rare to see a woman such as you alone, ya know." He searched my face for some agreement, but not receiving any, he lowered his eyes to the ground. "Ye 'ave no relation to go to?"

I didn't answer. I knew the place he spoke about. The rooms were in the same place I had gone begging to as a child. It was the only eatery in town as far as I could remember. It was not a great place for a single woman at all.

"I know that place." I looked down my nose at him and stiffened. He was a boy, not much older than I was. "Is there no other accommodation in this village?" I pretended that I couldn't believe it. "I want to be safe."

"No, mum. There are no public rooms for hire here. You will find room with your employer, or he will find room for you. Do you know yer employer?" he asked, trying not to seem too interested.

"An accountant in town I wish to approach. So I will not reveal his name until I do so. Thank you, young sir." I reminded him of our age and class differences. He was a little too curious for his own good. A bell rang from behind the door where I had listened so long ago.

"That be the father, if you will. I must serve his needs." He looked toward the door with a scrunched-up face. All the openness of youth suddenly drained from him. "Do not hesitate to call on us in the future. Father Peck enjoys lively discussion with all people." He fled toward the door and paused there to give me a tip of his head.

I gave a swift dip of my knees and a smile of understanding on my face. He turned and disappeared behind the door.

I walked briskly out of the kirk. The soft ruffling of my skirts caught my attention. I had never worn undergarments such as this. The sound was not soothing. It made me want to hurry. Perhaps someone was behind me. I looked but, no, it was only myself in lady's clothing.

Faithful Murray sat much as I had left him. It must have been difficult to maintain the illusion out in the open like that. I hurried and climbed into the cart without stepping on my clothes.

"Turn around and go back up the street to the eatery. They have rooms to let, the only rooms in the village."

"Yes, milady."

The cart swiveled around easily, and the old horse trundled back up High Street. We were once again in the thick of human and animal business.

"Shall I go in thar wit ye?" Murray asked without shifting.

"Would a hired driver accompany me into such an establishment?"

"Only if he was na' certain of his pay, so I'll wait til you come out. Easier to hold the illusion," he said as he turned his head slightly. He wasn't quite looking at me.

I wasn't sure if it were because it was too hard to hold the image if he moved or if it were the way a driver would act.

I climbed down with some difficulty, with long skirts getting underfoot. It would be better for my own image to seem as old and unfit as I was portrayed. I stood in the road and neatened myself, patting down my skirts and trying to rewrap the wimple. It draped over my head and then went around my neck and covered up to my chin. No one saw the red hair I was covering, just my white face with small wrinkles etched into it. It was the first cloth of linen I had ever used.

Murray helped me to conjure it because I had never even touched linen before. Murray helped with the entire kit, from the kirtle to the over gown and girdle. I had no idea what a proper lady wore, but I knew that styles were fickle and changed with the breezes. According to Murray, my illusion would feel most comfortable in an earlier fashion than current. I wore the straight and long undergarment with the kirtle over that, which tied in the front.

The dark blue-dyed wool gown had a neck-covering bodice went over it all. The long sleeves were hanging, better to hide the hands with. The girdle was a wide leather belt I wore at the waist. It was more for decoration than use. The outer gown was cut to my form and tighter at the waist, but bloomed out around my hips. Current fashion was a more slender cut, but this suited my bigger body much better.

I took a step just as a bleating billy goat ran across my path. A young boy with a switch and a puppy jumping at his heels followed. Before my next step, I looked both ways as well as down, watching for traffic and the leavings of animals. Oxen-pulled carts loaded with wooden barrels and men walked by, laden with containers or packs of every sort. Merchants called out their wares from the doorways of their houses. It was a mass of noise and sound that I could not imagine getting used to.

I made my way to the open door of the establishment and walked into a large eating hall.

"G'day, milady!" the plump mistress called as she came running up. "What be yer desire?"

"What I desire is a room to let for two nights, if you please." I had to have an air of privilege. "I hear this be the only rooming house in the village."

"Yes, mum. That be right. But we are clean and safe, not to worry about that. There be only the one o' ya? Ye be wantin' a room to yer self?"

"Yes, please. What is the charge?"

"Do ya wants food and drink, mum? Or just a room?"

"A room with a bed, please. And a clean mattress and blanket. A lock on the door would be desirable."

"Yes, madam. That ye kin 'ave, not fer nothin' though. I usually 'ave two or three to a bed and four beds to a room, a couple pallets wit three to four more on the floor. Each one o' them pays a bawbee, and so for you, milady, it would twelve shillings a night, if you please." She scuffed her feet on the crusty dirt floor and looked down, a sure sign she was cheating me. It was only a few bawbee too much.

"Have you such a large and clean room with only one bed, a bowl of hot water for washing, and a towel for drying? With a lock on the door and no worries of bedbugs or fleas? I would pay extra for fresh bedcovers fer sure. What say ye?" I was enjoying this banter. "And for good service, I may be willing to pay an extra bawbee or two," I added with a slight smile.

"Yes, milady, it can be arranged. I'll put me boys to it right now. Donnie! Finn! We be needin' one bed in one room. The room that locks, ya know. Put the other beds in the other room, and I'll take care o' the rest."

Two men paused to hear the missus. They stared at me while she spoke. Then they nodded and ran up the stairs.

"Now about payment, milady."

I paid her price for two nights and then went out to pay Murray.

He had gotten off the cart and was leaning on the side of a wheel that was almost as tall as he was, even in his taller form. "You right, milady? That was a bit o'a long time. Hard negotiatin', me guesses. Now ya be owin' me one pound sterling, if ya please." He grinned and licked his lips.

"One pound!" I yelled. "That's usury fer sure!"

I winked and opened the little pouch at my girdle. I manifested a pound sterling between my fingers and thrust it out to Murray violently. "Here you are, you robber. Now off with you!" I reached over his shoulder and picked up my packet. It had some spare things, just for looks, and the letter of introduction.

Murray stood straight and took my other hand. "Take care, me Bernie," he whispered. "I'll be waitin' fer yer return. Be quick and safe. Call fer help if ya need." He touched my fingers to his lips, made a jump into the cart, lashed the horse with the reins, and, with a jolt, moved off into the hordes on High Street.

16

THE KIRK

"Yer room be ready, madam," the mistress called as I entered the hall. "Up the stairs and down to the end. The door be open fer ya."

I looked around the busy room. *Is anyone paying attention?* Most eyes were on their plates. Some were talking enthusiastically. I saw no interest in myself. But I was annoyed that my situation was announced to the realm. I gave her a glare as I trod up the steps.

There was a bolt on the inside of the door but no way to lock the room if I were out. The narrow bed was stuffed with straw. It seemed clean enough. I swept the room with a cleansing spray of magic and was confident, for the most part, I would be free of lice upon sitting or lying there. There was only a bed. I sat down, heavily feeling the full weight of what I was meant to do.

I knew I best get started as soon as I could, but I had no plan. My first thought was to go back and try to get an audience with the priest.

I don't want to befriend him. Maybe I could get an understanding of him. Does he really think there are witches? I'm a mage, not a witch, of course. I don't need spells and incantations.

Mine was a change of mind. It was understanding *qi*, like the rays of the sun, knowing how to manipulate the environment of space and the smallest particles. It meant knowing your mind too. Lou said anyone could do it. I didn't know why more people didn't know about it, except maybe we were better off without it. It didn't really matter; mage or witch. Neither was acceptable to the kirk or the simple people.

I had no idea what I was doing here. The only other person who could help me in the world was Lou. *Why did he abandon me? He might as well be dead.* As far as I knew, he was. I felt nothing from him, just like when my mum and da died. One moment, they were there, and the next, nowhere.

The bed was starting to feel comfortable, but I had work to do. I shook off the sadness and opened the small packet to let the insides be displayed. Some cheap hairpins and an under tunic I could sleep in was all I had. If someone wanted them, so be it. I could not lock the door from the outside, but I put a feeling of "stay out" around it, kind of like covering it with a blanket so no one could see it. Down the stairs and out the door, I went in a confident pose, straight-backed and forward looking. I headed for the kirk, feeling not so confident about my mission and myself.

As always, the kirk felt cold and dank. Someone had left some candles burning at the back of the hall in front of the laird's bench. I could smell the oily smell of their smoke as it burned and wax dripped down the candlesticks. I walked across the room to the wooden door. I heard nothing behind it.

I scratched and called, "Haloo!" My voice sounded faint and

childlike. I remembered Cullan rapping on the door to his mother's room with his knuckles, so I tried that. It was much more forceful and demanding.

"Aye! Hold yer horses," a voice called from a distance. I heard a door shut and the scuffle of sandals on the cold, stone floor. "What be yer urgency?" The young acolyte opened the door. "Oh, it be you again. Pardon meself, madam. What kin I do fer ye?"

"I am to beg your pardon, sir." I did not know what to call him. He wasn't a father. "I came to visit with Father Peck, as ya told me earlier. You said he would take visitors. Is he within that I might enjoy an evening visit?"

"Ah yes, but he is now taking his meal."

"Would it bother his digestion if I intruded for some stimulating conversation? I bring introduction from the bishop of St. Andrews. And I do not know if I will have time again, as I intend to start my employment soon." I looked expectantly into his face and projected a whole hearted enthusiasm for the so-called stimulating conversation.

"I will go and ask the good father what his preference might be. Please wait here." He shut the door in front of me, and I could hear his sandals scraping on the way back down the hall. A door opened and shut.

It seemed like a very long time. I was just thinking I'd been forgotten when the acolyte made his way back to me. "Very well, madam. Father Peck looks forward to your company tonight. Please follow me."

We walked past the kitchen, where my mum met with Dougal, but I didn't have time to peer into it. We continued down a hall to an open door and stepped in. The room was well lit with oil lamps scattered around. The walls were lined with shelves, and they were stacked with paper scrolls.

Father Peck was sitting behind a large desk with inkpots and writing tools littered here and there, but at this moment, a feast covered most of the desk. I could see this man was highly regarded just from the repast of his table. There were several kinds of meats: fish, poultry, and a leg of lamb. A large, crusty loaf of bread had a prominent spot on the table with cheese and jellies and a broth of meat stew with carrot and onion bobbing around inside. The aroma was delicious, and though I had not eaten, I could not have swallowed a bite. This was the priest of my childhood.

As far as I could see, he hadn't changed. He was much more interested in himself and the food placed before him than the woman who stood in front of him. Behind his head on a large cupboard was a silver cross. It sat like a sword sunk into the wood of the board and sparkled in the light of the lamps. It hurt my eyes to look at it, and yet I could hardly move them from it. I felt my stomach turn as I remembered the sound of crunching bones and my mum's screams when the cross came down on her upraised wrist. My hands tightened at my sides. Now was not the time to remember the past. I must keep moving.

"Good evening, madam. Forgive me if I do not greet you properly. Please take this chair. And would you enjoy some wine? I think we have enough for a half glass or so. Is that right, William?" His hands and face glistened with grease. He looked to be enjoying his meal and not inclined to share.

"Yes, Father. This is Katherine Fergus, sir, from Edinburgh, with greetings from Bishop Winchester. I'll get the wine." He backed out of the door, and I took a high-backed chair in front of the desk.

"Thank you, sir. Uh, Father," I said shyly. "Since William suggested you might enjoy some conversation, I have looked forward to facing you."

"And would you have word from our bishop, John Winchester,

milady?" He took a large bite of bread, and before chewing it, he put a piece of roast chicken into his mouth. The chicken carcass sat on a plate in its own grease. The skin was cooked to a crispy brown, and the priest chewed with small, fast movements. He eyed me curiously. He probably thought he had me and was going to throw me out. William did not return quickly with my wine.

"Did ya not hear, Father? Bishop Winchester of Moray died in April. That be only four months ago. I did not hear it myself until June. I have a word from the bishop of St. Andrews, James Kennedy. I'm afraid Brother William misinterpreted the message I have brought. It is nothing but an introduction from the bishop. I was allowed this blessing due to the connection between our families. My own grand mum was a member of Clan Carrick, our family from Ayreshire in the south."

As I spoke, I retrieved the small scroll from the pouch at my belt. Looking at his greasy fingers, I unrolled it. I didn't want to give it to him, and just as I was about to, William walked in and placed a half glass of wine in front of me.

"Excuse me, William. Would you show this paper to the father?" I asked sweetly.

He understood immediately as a young man of fastidious appearance. He held the small page open while the greasy father read the writing. The priest read with rapid chewing and swallowing. He took a gulp of his wine, and William left to get more.

"You be widowed, I see. I thought so. And have you a plan fer yourself, or will you move on from Forresgem? Says you be a scholar of sorts. You read, write, and know your numbers. You be an unusual woman, I'd say. How come you by this training?"

Some grease or spittle slid out the side of his mouth. He pried a drumstick off the chicken carcass with a pop, and with both elbows on the table and both hands on the morsel, he chewed away at the bulb of meat. I took a sip from the goblet of wine. It was a fine red wine, probably donated by the laird. Murray had taught me well.

"My father was invited to teach the acolytes at St. Salvator. He practiced teaching on my mum and myself. He said, if he could teach a young girl how to read, write, and number, he could teach anyone. He also taught me to read in British and French," I said, feigning a sense of pride.

"Did he train you in Latin?" The priest jabbed the naked leg bone in the air like a knife.

"No, my lord priest. He knew that would be against the will of the kirk. Women are not to be made privy to the secrets of the Latin kirk. I had enough to do learning what I do know." I smiled at him. He would have to take my word for it.

He sunk back in his chair, now eyeing the pulpy white carcass of a boiled fish on a platter. With both hands, he tore a fist-sized chunk of bread off the loaf and pulled the platter of fish to him. I sipped the wine daintily. As a lady, I was not to drink too quickly, nor with too much enjoyment. It was a good vintage, not Scottish for sure. Perhaps French.

I watched as he took a large piece of the flaky fish in his fingers and laid it over the piece of bread. He put it up to his face, eyeing it with half-closed lids. With a smile of contentment, he put the whole piece of bread and fish in his mouth. Soon I could see he was having trouble chewing the huge bite of food. It was so big that he had trouble moving it around in his mouth.

His eyes flew open, his cheeks puffed out, and he tried harder and harder to grasp the lump between his teeth. He tried to swallow, but I could see this wasn't possible. I knew he was in danger but knew not what to do. I couldn't be seen to let him choke, although I wanted to.

When he grabbed at his throat and opened his mouth to release some of the food, I jumped up and opened the door.

"William!" I screamed. "Come now! Come now!" I had to make some attempt to save him. I might be accused of murder.

I dashed over to the priest, who was making desperate squeaks, his air restricted. I pounded his back with some force but knew I should not be touching him, and I feared to hurt him. Suddenly the door flew open, and William dashed in. He saw me pound the father's back and quickly moved to push me away. But he had no better remedy. He rolled the gagging man to the floor.

"Save him! Save him!" I screamed.

His gagging was weaker. He was dying.

"Please leave, lady. I will help the father to his bed."

The man lay on the floor convulsing as I backed out of the door. I fled to my room, knowing the priest would be dead before I got there.

In my room, I could not rest. I paced back and forth. My mind was racing. The priest was dead, and I had nothing to do with it. I was confused. His death from gagging was not near what I'd had in mind. But I must admit that I'd had nothing in mind. How would I kill someone without being caught? I could not have done it while William rested in a room nearby. It was done for me by the priest himself. *Now what should I do?*

I paced three steps up and three steps back. In my pacing, I felt the channels of power in my body opening and closing, *qi* moving through, wanting to move my body. I dared not, in case I made a noise.

In the wee hours of the morn, a scratch came on my door. I was sitting silently on my bed, as Lou had trained me.

The scratch came louder, and a deep voice said, "Madam."

I quickly unpinned my hair. "One moment, please," I replied in a startled, high-pitched voice. I disheveled my garments and threw the wimple over my head like a shawl, trying to look as if I had been asleep.

A tall man with sun-streaked brown hair and a bandage on one shoulder stood in the doorway. He was clean and had shaved, and I knew him as the knight whose wound I had treated.

"Madam, you are under arrest for the murder of the parish priest, Father Peck."

"What are you saying, my lord? Murder? I saw the man choking on a large bite of fish and bread. I did not know what to do. So I called out. The acolyte, William, told me to leave. The good father was not dead when I left."

Panic began to set in. I felt hot sweat gathering upon me, and my skin flushed. The knight gave a raise of his eyebrow and looked at me sideways. *Is that recognition I see in his face or disbelief?* He appeared unmoved.

"The charges are murder by witchcraft or spellbinding, milady. Best get your things. You'll be moving to the gaol until the sheriff arrives from Inverness."

He was without a care. It was only a job for him. *Is he the new gaol man?* All my memories of my poor mum came flooding in. I almost laughed a hysterical peal, but instead gripped myself in my own arms and began to shake violently.

The knight stood his ground. He seemed without sympathy, cold and bored. Under his hard gaze, I felt all the blood leave my face in a rush, and I fainted.

"Is she daid?" I heard the mistress ask.

"No," my captor replied. "Is she paid up fer today?"

To my great surprise, the woman answered, "Aye, she is, and a fine person she is too, Craig. Very generous. No witch that I could tell and you can give that word to her accuser. What did ye do to her?"

"Not a thing, Milly. She fainted dead away."

"Thar, ya see? She hain't no witch. She would ha bespelled ya before she opened the door for ye."

I was slung over his good shoulder like a bag of turnips. One of his hands held my skirt over my legs, and my head hung down his back. I could smell the odor of the man, a mix of sweat and grass hay with some oily soap mixed in. But I was not in a mood to linger there. I wasn't sure I could walk to the gaol though.

"Let me go, sir," I mumbled childlike. It was like being carried by my da when I was a wee thing.

"Oh yes, Craig, let the madam have some dignity wouldja, man?" Milly seemed concerned. I loved her from that moment.

"Of course, I'm only doin' my job after all," he said gruffly.

Neither one seemed particularly afraid of me.

Milly brought a stool over. "I'll fetch us some tea. You can stay a few minutes, Craig. It's too early for customers. I be only a moment."

She bustled to the kitchen, and I could hear coals being prodded and the clack of cups. Sir Knight seemed inclined to wait. I wasn't going anywhere.

I put my face in my hands and suddenly remembered the wimple. He had it in his hand. I pointed to it, and he thrust it at me. My red hair hung in long strands around my shoulders. I had nothing to tie it with, so I just pushed it back and affixed the wimple in the proper fashion. I tried to straighten my rumpled clothing and regain some of myself while I checked the feel of my illusion. It was part of me now; I would have no trouble maintaining it.

"I am nothing like a witch," I said with a sniff.

Milly returned and handed me a cloth she had dampened in warm water. I was so grateful to be able to press it against my eyes and face. The tears started to flow.

"Thar, thar, dearie. No need to cry just yet. Craig will take good care o' ye." She stroked my back with her plump and strong hand.

"This is some kind of mistake," I pleaded between sobs. "How could anyone think that I am a witch? I have an introduction paper from the bishop of St. Andrews, a family acquaintance."

"And where is this paper, madam?" Craig asked with growing interest. "This will help your case greatly."

I paused to think. I had left it in the priest's room. In fact, I did not remember getting it back from William.

"Oh no," I said slowly. "William held the scroll for the father to read. His hands were greasy from his food. William must have left it on the father's table. I fear I don't recall him giving it back to me."

"I'll look over the desk again," he said.

"The father was pushed to the floor by William. Perhaps the small scroll fell to the floor," I interrupted. I was beginning to see a problem. "Is it possible that William might be the murderer?" I felt like I might be given a blow for my disrespect, but it just came out.

"No, no," said Milly, shaking her white-capped head. "Them two are like father and son. William served the father faithfully and with love."

I wasn't so sure about that.

17

THE SHERIFF

It was still early in the morn. No one had business in the village before the sun. So I was able to walk unknown to the gaol. Craig walked slightly behind me. In case I was to try to run, I supposed he could grab me. He did not know I possessed a fighting skill that could have laid him low with no one knowing or believing.

I was slowly regaining my wits and feeling my strength again. The initial shock of being falsely accused of murder and then of being a witch was so unnerving that I couldn't think straight. My body had almost given up right there in the faint. *How could this happen to me? I did not even take the first step in my revenge. In fact, someone beat me to it!* I couldn't even enjoy this new development. I did not want to kill Craig. I would soon be meeting the sheriff. He was coming to me. I could wait.

In one way, the Forresgem gaol was not unlike my own beloved cave. It was made of stone. It was much smaller, of course, and had a cobbled stone floor. There was one small window. More light came in from the bars in the solid wood door and my own private light helped a little. There was a low wooden bench that the inmate could sleep on and be up off the cold and clammy floor, which became infested with rats and other small animals at night. The gaoler's office was beyond the cell door and up a short flight of stairs on the other side of another solid door. When that door was closed, no sound came into the cell.

Craig took my arm and walked me down the steps to the dark cell. A firebrand burned on either side of the door, and it let some light and warmth into the space.

"I am sorry; lady, but I must leave you here now. I promise I will find the wee scroll you mentioned. I will speak with you when I return." I sat on the thin bench as he slowly turned and walked out.

The door creaked like a pig being slaughtered as he pulled it shut. The bolt clanged with a sharp grate as it slid into place, and I could hear the scuff of his boots as he climbed the stairs. The upstairs door swung closed, and its thud was like the last thudding beat of my heart. *Was all lost? Was my life forfeit, for nothing? What would Lou do?*

I stood up and began to walk in a circle. My mystical light was enhanced by the flickering brands in the hall beyond my cell. The window was high and blackened with dirt. The light shone through like a small rent in one's skirts.

Around and around I went. In the doing of it my mind calmed, and my confidence returned. I did have some magic, and I could create illusion. I thought of fire and felt the heat, and just for fun, I jabbed it out of my fingertips like bolts of lightning. It was impressive, but it had no substance. It might convince someone though, and then he'd know I was a witch for sure. It made me laugh, and the sound of it reverberated off the dull stone walls with the eerie trill of the bean nighe, a keening screech announcing a death to come. In my current disguise, I might even be confused with the little old washerwoman who knew when a person was going to die.

It wasn't long, as time goes, before I heard the swoosh of the upstairs door opening and the slice of the bolt moving in the cell door. I stood in the middle of my small circle when Craig entered. He didn't look at me.

"Follow me, madam." He turned and walked out.

At the top of the stairs, the room was flooded with light. Doors and windows were open, and I could see the afternoon was a glorious blue and green of a late summer. My sixteenth birthday was soon to pass. My chances of survival seemed slim.

Craig shut the door and motioned to a table and chair. I sat, and he dragged a small bench over and sat too. He produced a cloth that contained bread and cheese and poured out two cups of watered wine.

"This, from Milly," he said bluntly.

We ate in silence. Even our chewing was quiet. Craig drank down his wine in one violent tip of his head.

"I did na' find your wee scroll from the bishop. I was tolt a full different story from Brother William."

I was not surprised. It was his word against mine, and of course, my word was nothing.

"Then he lies," I said.

My eyes were bright with fury, but I remained calm. He had destroyed the scroll. I was sure. There was no sense considering trying to find it. Maybe I could scare him into the truth. It would be difficult from my imprisonment.

"One or the other of you do. That is fer sure. He being a man o' God puts him in the right. I don' have to point out." His shoulders slumped. "I have a mind to side with Milly on this. I just can't see you as an evil witch."

"Can you see any woman as an evil witch, I ask you? Have you seen the women they choose to make witches of?" I leaned over the table with my hands open in front of me. I wanted to draw him in, to have him by my side, to touch him. "I am not a witch. There are no witches."

He nodded his head. "I have never seen one."

"What did William tell you?"

"He said he came running to the room when he heard shouting. Once there, he saw you making stabbing motions at the father's back. When he pushed you away, the father fell to the floor and died. You ran away." He looked in my face as if the truth could be written upon it.

"He came running because I opened the door and yelled for help. The father was choking on the large piece of bread and fish he had just put in his mouth. The only thing I could think to do was pound his back, hoping he would disgorge what was choking him. That's what William saw when he came in. I stepped back, and he pushed the priest onto the floor and told me to leave. If I had killed him, would I come back to my room? No, I would have fled."

He nodded slowly. "What were you doing there anyway?"

"I was there for conversation. I met William in the kirk earlier, and he said to come back anytime. The father enjoyed stimulating conversation. I had come here to find employment with an accountant by the name of Ferrand MacTigue. That's why I had the letter from the bishop."

Craig stiffened when I mentioned MacTigue. "That be my da."

Just for a wee moment, hardly a space, I lost my composure. Craig didn't notice, but I did. *His da! I am closer to Janet than I knew.*

"Oh my goodness." I shifted in my seat and feigned smoothing my tunic. My wimple, long forgotten, hung over my shoulders. I had an urge to put it on, but it was too late now. "I am sure the possibility of that happening now are naught. In fact, I don't think I will be getting out of this alive. I have no proof and no advocate. These trials are swift, and St. Andrews is several days from here. There is no one to stand for me." My voice got higher as the panic of my position overcame me, and I began to weep.

"The sheriff will arrive tomorrow. I will stand for ya. Milly will too."

"But to no avail. I have not even been in this town for more than a day," I sobbed. "I never met Milly before midday yesterday and you this morn before the sun. My position is dire." I was beginning to shake.

"You should take some rest, and I'll continue to question William." He stood up and went out of the room. When he returned, he had a feather-stuffed blanket. "Ye can use the bench for your pallet. This will warm you."

Back down to the cell I went. I supposed it could be a safe place for me once the word got out, which it surely would sooner or later.

The firebrands were out. No light came through the door window, but I could see. I moved the bench so it wasn't facing the door, and if light came through, it didn't shine down on me. And then I sat.

Hours later, I heard the soft opening and closing of the upstairs door. A gentle ray of light pierced the barred window in the cell door, and a slow scraping of the bolt told me the door would very soon open. When it did open, a long-fingered hand holding a candle plate came into the darkness of my cell. The candle waved around, casting a feeble light, and the person holding it ventured in.

My pallet was right next to the door, so I was behind the person when he walked in. I was sitting there watching as the tall, thin man entered the room. He came in slowly but boldly. He was not afraid of a witch. He didn't believe in witches. The same sheriff who had murdered my mother turned to face me.

I let my old body and red hair illusion go. I was myself. In that moment, in the dull light of a candle, the sheriff saw what I wanted him to see. He gasped with a rasping intake of breath and almost dropped the candle.

"You!" he said in a low roar. "You were quite clearly dead. In fact, you were mostly dead before you were put in that barrel. How?" After he succumbed to a momentary chill of fear, he drew the candle up and down for a better look at me. He was definitely a brave man.

"Sir, you must be referring to my mum. It is she you abused and then murdered." I drew myself up in front of him. Like a cat, I felt every bone and muscle in my body relax in a tense readiness. He did not have a weapon that I could see.

With his confidence returned, he shut the cell door. He could not conceive of a situation he would not walk away from.

"This is much better than I was expecting. Youthful flesh is much more exciting. In fact, I can hardly wait to get my hands on you. Come here, lass. Make it easy on yer self. You'll be riding the barrel to the witch's stone soon enough." He had a strange look in his eyes, and the smile on his face was more like the growling muzzle of a mad dog.

"Let me help you with yer clothes." He lunged at me with the candle, trying to light my skirts on fire. "Don't worry. I'll be quick. A little pain will be nothin' compared to the knife and the barrel."

I easily avoided both the fire and his grasp. I was a cat playing with a mouse. I smiled an evil smile as I pulled at a lace on my over tunic. I enticed him into my cat circle, daring and teasing him. I turned up the heat in the room. Licking my lips, I loosened the laces until my bodice hung open and the kirtle was exposed.

"Ah, I see you want it! Yes, you do." In a bold move, he threw off his overcoat and searched for a place to put the candle plate.

"Here," I said in a smooth, enticing voice, "let me take care of that."

I put balls of light all around the cell. He was entranced. His prey was as good as his.

He strode boldly up to me and reached out his hand. Lou had always said it was the opponent who should make the first move. Every action was based on what the opponent did. The sheriff grabbed my arm and pulled with a violent yank.

I let him pull. He was expecting some resistance, but I was as light as a feather. He stumbled and took a step back. As he went, I climbed up his body, first stepping hard on the top of his soft leather boot and then kicking a knee. He stumbled forward as I made another kick at his manhood. Screaming, he doubled over as I followed the spiraling swirl of the kick with my elbow catching him on the side of the head and the jaw. In a sudden release of piercing energy, I smashed his nose with my palm. He hit the cobblestones headfirst.

No one could hear his screams. He had made sure of that before he came in. I circled his writhing body. I was sure his nose was broken. It was a bloody mass, maybe his jaw too. He had bitten his tongue and was bleeding from his mouth and the back of his head. The blood puddled onto the cobblestones.

"I want you to meet your devil," I hissed. "Tonight you go to hell."

He had stopped screaming and lay curled up, unable to move or talk. His breath came in harsh gulps through his gaping bloody mouth. I could find no sympathy. I would have helped a dying cat, but this man was below my caring. I wanted him to suffer.

I stood over him and began to replay my own mum's final moments. Only, it was himself that was in the barrel. I entered his mind with the mental pictures of the masked executioner shutting the lid on him. He was in total darkness with only seeping dots of light around the barrel slats. Then he heard a loud booming and felt a vibration reverberate around him. A newly sharpened tip of a blade suddenly pierced the wood and scraped past his ribs. It drew blood. New screams arose from the body on the floor, guttural shrieks gurgling with blood. He could not move; he believed he was trapped in the barrel.

Again and again, I made him feel the fright of a blade coming through. His screams became weaker until they stopped. I envisioned the executioner moving the barrel onto its side and shoving it down the hill, hearing a roar of approval from the crowd. The man in the barrel was battered and sliced by the blades. He careened off the white rocks and flew through the air, slamming down, over and over until he rolled finally into the last boulder. The barrel cracked open, spilling its contents, which was him, broken, bleeding, and undoubtedly dead.

The man on the floor was not dead. He thought he was, and I would not do anything to change his mind. I began to heal him, not only because I could not leave him bloodied on the cell floor, but also because I wanted him to suffer. With all my minor skills of magic, I slowly repaired his jaw, broken nose, and tongue. He would have some trouble eating for a day or two, but it would be minor. In his fall, he cracked his skull.

All of this, I put back. I erased all traces of blood and repaired torn clothing. I laid his coat over him, and I put myself back into my illusion of Kathryn and sat on the bench covered over in Craig's warming blanket. I gave him the witch's experience, wanting him to live it over and over. I was sure it would change him. My energy was spent.

A gentle hand shook my shoulder. "Lady Kathryn. Kathryn, wake now." Craig was kneeling in front of me, looking most concerned. "What went on here? Are you right?"

I blinked. I had fallen asleep and felt a bit confused. *What is he doing here?*

"Come, lady. What's your story? Something very strange I'll wager. I have tea upstairs."

That got me up, but I didn't want to speak. *Where is the sheriff?* I knew I must let the opponent move first. I hobbled stiffly up the stairs. I didn't have to pretend I was old.

"When I got here earlier, both doors were open. You were sittin' all wrapped up on your bench, sound asleep. How did you get the door open?" He poured some tea into a cup.

Its steam caressed the skin on my face as I brought it to my mouth. "The sheriff was here. Did you not know?" I asked in a small, wavering voice.

"His horse is still out front. He must have come in late after I was abed." Craig looked puzzled.

"Yes, it was late. He shut both doors so you could not hear."

The sheriff was probably gathering reinforcements and coming to accuse me of witchery. *How could I have been so stupid to let him go? I've broken one of Lou's rules for fighting, fight to kill.*

"He began to question me about witches." I started to sob. "He made threats and was very excited. I thought my life was over right then. He grabbed my arm and pulled me to him. I thought he was going to kill me. I will tell ye, Craig, that, if anyone looked more than a demon then he did last night, then ... then ... he should be kilt. The man was in a rage. He pushed me down and then went tromping out. I did not even know the door was open." I was ashamed to say it. I did not believe in demons. I broke into a torrent of tears.

"But why did he leave you there all by yer self with the doors open? Did he declare you innocent?"

"It seems so." My tears slowed. The thought had not come to me.

Why would he leave the doors unlocked? He went out in such a rage. Perhaps he might be going to get a weapon to kill me himself.

"Where did he go?" Craig got up and went into the next room.

I could hear some dishes clack. I thought about stealing the sheriff's horse and running away. But I stayed. I had to follow this through. Not having a plan meant being ready for whatever outcomes may arise. Craig returned, bringing a half-eaten chicken carcass, bread, and cheese.

"The chicken is from last eve's meal, if you're interested. It still tastes good." He was not a man of hidden agendas. He was forthright and honest.

"I am hungry. Thank you for your kindness." I wiped my eyes on my sleeves, and I broke a piece of bread off the loaf and a bit of cheese to go with it.

"I have a mind to let you go; however, there is the accuser still to be dealt with."

"You know he is using me this way because he is the murderer, of course," I said in between chews. "What if we found out that the good father simply died of choking? That is what I assumed. Can ye tell William you examined the body and could find nothing that showed murder or witchcraft? That possibly I was pounding his back to release stuck food?"

"Hmm, aye. That might work, if I were willing to let a murderer go." He smiled at me.

"Or let an innocent person die a witch's death." I popped a bit of cheese in my mouth. It melted in salty sourness. I felt a little better after the food.

"I will try this plan of yours, and then I will keep a very close eye on William."

"I'm sure he is already packing to leave the area." I daintily picked a small piece of meat to try. It was dry and inedible.

"I be meanin' to ask ye. Have we met before? Sometimes I feel something familiar about you."

"I have no knowin' of that," I said, looking more closely at him. "Who is your mum?"

"Her name was Janet. It is not a name I speak very much. She left me da in disgrace, riding off with a simple priest."

"Have you an older sister then?" I queried.

"No, it be just me. My little brother is laid to his grave now." He turned is face to the window just for a moment.

"Where is your mum now?" I looked at my hands in my lap, checking for dirt under the fingernails.

"Och! As far as I know, she's in Edinburgh, still with that bastard Dougal. She may be rotting in her grave for all I care." He looked at me, daring me to say something about her in a kindly way.

Instead I said, "I once had a cousin of the de Bruce clan who lived hereabouts. He was a crofter for the Laird MacTigue. Ye may know of him. His name was Duncan. His wife was Bridget, and he had a daughter. She would be, oh, about sixteen now. Her name was Bernadette. When my cousin died, I attended the funeral, but after that, I had no contact with the wife. We lived so far apart, and she was a crofter's wife. Our lives were so much different. She was an amiable woman. I wonder whatever happened to her."

"I do believe me mum had some contact with this family, but I had already gone off to serve King James. My brother followed me. Perhaps this is the familiarity I feel." He looked blankly at me, disappointed.

"Now that you have reminded me, I would like to find Bridget. We would have good conversation," I said brightly.

"Bridget MacTigue, the name is known to me. It's not a good ending poor Bridget came to. She was the last woman to ride the barrel to the witch's stone, if I recall. I was not home, but me da told the story later."

"Oh my!" I exclaimed. "And to think I very narrowly followed her. What became of her lovely child, Bernadette? How long ago did this happen?" Tears came easily to my eyes again.

"Did Bernadette have raven black hair and a slight build, very small?" He leaned forward, eager for some information.

"Well, yes. The one time I saw her. She had very white skin and black hair, and she was small for a girl of nine or ten years. Her da had just died. Bridgett had a babe in her arms then."

"Where is she now? I want to see her again." He jumped up and leaned over the table as if he would take to his horse at any minute to go searching.

"I have not an idea," I said, straightening on the bench. "Her parents are dead. Maybe she is raising her young sister somewhere. Perhaps she is married to a crofter with a babe of her own. I'm sorry. I do not know."

I did not know what to think about this man. "When did you see the girl last?" I wanted to hear his impression of our meeting and why he was so wanting to see me again.

"It was about two weeks ago. I wasn't quite lost in the laird's woods, ya know, but I would have said so if someone asked. I was just getting home after my years fighting for the king. He did give me knighthood after all. I knew a small pond in a creek up there, and I took me horse up for a drink. I was wounded in the right shoulder and pretty sure I'd die due to the infection that was beginning. You can't get good doctoring in the field.

"My horse, Curly be his name, was taking a long draught when I looked up, and there across the pond was a lovely girl, skirts hiked up around her knees, feet dangling in the pond, and sound asleep on a mossy outcrop. I had seen nothing but wretched camp followers and barmaids for my whole time with the king, so I was entranced. She awoke to my staring but calmly put herself to rights and stood up to go. She had the most beautiful long, black locks and white skin. I thought sure she was of the Good People.

"She said she was a crofter getting a nap in and would be off to work. I remember telling her to stay a moment more, and then I blacked out. I believe I fell off me horse and slept through the day and night with that girl tending to my wound. She cleaned it and put a drawing poultice on it, built a small shelter over me, and got food and drink off my horse to place near me. I have not seen her since." He paused for a long time. "I can't get her out of my head, and I want to see her again."

"Did she not tell you her name or croft?" I asked in surprise.

"No, I feinted dead away. We didn't get beyond our own surprise of meeting in the woods." He shook his head and then looked up at me as if there were something I could do. I looked around to avoid his pleading gaze.

"I can make inquiries, sir, but I have to tell you, if I get out of this custody, I will be disappearing for a much gentler climate. This one here, I find much too hot."

"I understand," he said as he stood up. "I best be goin' to see our good friend, William. Perhaps I can make him see the error he has committed. I am again putting you back in the cell. If the sheriff should return and finds you ambling about the place, he may be unhappy with me."

"Aye," I replied with a sigh. "That be the truth of it. Please do lock both doors and take the keys. I do not want any unwelcomed guests without protection."

I half-expected the sheriff to return with hate in his mind and murder in his eyes. But knowing there wasn't anything I could do about it now, I sat on my bench, wrapped up in my warm blanket, and waited and worried. *If I had killed him in my cell, how would I have removed the body? I haven't perfected my magic. Now that he'd had the experience and lived through it, is he out proclaiming my witchery to everyone?*

Mine would be a huge killing. But I would take him with me when the time came. If all were lost, I would make sure he would never abuse another innocent woman again. Something in his spirit was wrong. He was the closest thing to a demon I could imagine. Perhaps his world was a hell like Mum's telling of Dante's hell, and he was only acting out his part, bringing hell to others.

My musings took me late into the night, and I finally fell into a still sleep. Dreamless and solid, I would have been just as content to remain that way, but I awoke to the clang of the latch and Craig bounding in, success beaming on his face.

"My Lady Fergus, I proclaim you free of any charges and free to go." He had a big smile on his face and wide, expectant eyes.

I got up slowly, working out the stiffness in my muscles and bones. "My lord that is grand news. Our friend William must have seen the error of his ways?"

"Aye and, how accusing an innocent person of witchcraft would become a sin on his own shoulders. He may have been able to help the father. It is for him to know, and just his knowin' of it might be worse than if I accused him of murder. He will live with that curse and be sure of hell when he dies." He winked at me, and I took his hands in mine.

"Thank you for your belief in me, Sir Craig. But what of the sheriff?" I was mostly feeling free, but the apparition of the hate-filled man haunted me, and I shivered to think that he was still out there.

"Come upstairs. We'll break our fast and talk. Then I'll send you back to Milly's, where your room is waiting for you."

18

A MEETING

I followed Sir Craig up the stairs and into the living quarters of the gaol. He was a fine cook, and he created such a repast that I thought of Murray's simple but delicious feasts. We had boiled eggs with a pork shoulder and heated bread, complete with butter and oat porridge. For afterwards, there was some spiced tea and honey.

He said that the sheriff had disappeared. He had sent searchers out looking since he realized he'd gone without his horse. There were no armed men coming to get me, and there was no one to accuse me. I was free to go. He did have one request, that I would find Bernadette and give him leave to see her again.

This was what was dwelling in my mind as I sat on my straw bed in Milly's let room. I wanted to flee and to flee soon. I couldn't get the demon sheriff off my mind. If the sheriff were not missing but finding people to press for my death, I needed to disappear. I wanted to produce Bernadette, and that was for sure. I wanted to talk to Craig as myself. I was in danger of falling in love with him as not myself. He was a kind and good man, just the kind I could love and live with if I were to have the kind of life my mum had hoped for, one protected and a higher class than what I had known at the croft.

Being a knight, Craig would have been given a piece of land for his troubles. Also, asa knight, he might be called to battle for the king or, if not battle, any number of jobs the king might need someone for: tax collector, arbitration between crofters, or even temporary sheriff. He would be a good provider.

I sat for awhile, making up impossible stories with Craig as their subject until I remembered that I could never live a normal life. I could not find love and happiness and grow to old age with children and wee bairns all about. What folly my mind made up. Whatever guaranteed love and happiness anyway? Plenty of people married and had families but never found happiness. Craig's own mum looked for happiness with another man, upsetting her son and her husband, not to mention committing murder. I was meant to bring revenge and to fulfill a bargain with the Good People, a bargain I was now convinced I could not fulfill. This thought I put away for later. *First things first.*

I knew I would have Bernie meet with Craig. I wanted to know more about Janet. *What was she like, and why would she fight so hard for one man that she would ruin her family and destroy mine?* Then I would kill her. At least I would want to kill her. I wasn't so sure I could.

The next day, I told Craig I would find Bernadette and arrange a meeting for him at Milly's. That made him happy.

Two days later, I had found her. I told him she was an indentured servant to someone whose name and location I could not reveal. Bernie herself said not to tell him so he would not go there without invitation. She lived well enough but worked hard and long and so would not be able to meet him until evening. She would only meet him in a public house, and that would be Milly's, in a public room with myself and Milly nearby.

Of course he agreed. But Lady Fergus would be lying in her bed ill, according to my plan, and Milly would be the custodian.

As soon as I finished telling Craig the news, I found Milly in her kitchen. I sat heavily on a stool and pulled the wimple off my head. I took on a masque of tiredness that turned to illness as I sat there.

"Wot! Ye ain't verra well, Missus Fergus. I see it on yer face. Kin I do anythin' fer ya? Then ye be off fer yer bed." Milly was quite sure she knew what I needed.

"Yes, thank you, Milly. I believe I have a touch of sour stomach. I will take to my bed. I need to ask a favor of you on behalf of my young niece." I kept my voice low and put some small pain into it.

"Yes, mum. Wotever ya need, just ask me." Milly sat opposite me, resting her bulk on another small stool.

"It seems that the gaoler, Sir Craig, has a fancy fer the child."

"Oh no! The truth?" Her hands flew up to cover her mouth. A wonderful piece of gossip it would be.

"Yes, but Milly, you must first promise to not tell a single soul, or I will call off this meeting. Promise?" I tried to act stern and sick.

"Sir Craig is one of the most eligible bachelors in Moray Shire! This be news. How can I keep it?" she whined.

"You must. This is just a first meeting. The girl is very shy. She can't afford public talk. She could lose her position. And then what would she do?"

"She would marry our Craig! That's wot she'd do!" Milly was so excited that she could hardly keep still.

"But Milly, please think. She would be forced. And what if after a first visit she didn't want to marry him? Maybe it would be a bad coupling." I gave a little feeble cough to remind her I was sick.

"Ah, you 'ave the right of it. Very well, but if there is a second meet, I don't need permission to let go the news. Many a young and not so young woman has been interested in Craig. He should'a been married off by now." She shook her head as if it were her fault Craig was not married.

I could see she had tried to find him a wife. "Milly, I am too ill to accompany them. So I am asking if you would watch over the girl. They must not go out alone. I require that their visit be brief and in view of yourself, preferably in your public hall. I don't want anything to ruin my niece's current situation. I will ask her to come to my room when they are done." I looked with tired, sick eyes into Milly's face to get some verification from her that she was listening and understood. "She'll be here later today."

She looked at me carefully. She seemed to be checking the severity of my health through furrowed eyes. She stood up. "Yes, lady. Now repair to yer bed. You do look enfeebled. I will bring ya a healing tea me mum taught me to make. Would ya like a bit o'this mutten broth? I think ya should. It will keep ya strong."

I nodded my head and gave a feeble smile as I slowly stood to go. "Do you have a pinch or two of salt for the broth and a dollip of honey for the tea? I would be grateful." I hobbled over to the kitchen door. "G'night."

"I'll bring it meself, mum. Just a wee moment."

"Thank you," I said as I pushed out the door.

She did come in soon after I had taken to my bed. She shuttered the window and lit a candle to put on the hardwood floor. I appeared to be sleeping, so she put the bowl of food and the drink on the floor where I could reach it and left without waking me.

I pushed the lock with a force of *qi*. I had been practicing since I was back in my room. It was a little like magic in that I had to find the *energia* of the wooden bar. With a force matching that of the wood and enough mental power, I could move the bar to bolt the door. I had learned the concept in fighting with Lou but didn't put together that I could apply it to other things. Now I could lift things up. I could throw things, push things, and carry light things for a short distance without a touch. This was insignificant conjuring done with *energia*, not with the smallest particles.

I picked up the bowl as I sat up in bed. Without spilling a drop, it floated over to me. With magic, I produced some onion to float in the bowl along with a piece of bread and cheese. Now that was dinner. I sat on my bed with my back to the wall and ate. After dinner, I sipped the sweet tea and ate a small, rosy apple I conjured.

It was getting time for Bernie to arrive. I slipped out of bed, letting my illusion go as I went. A shiver of excitement went through me. I was looking forward to this meeting despite my constant reminders that a marriage to Craig was all wrong. It could never happen for his own well-being. I changed my tattered gown into a clean shift, and rather than go barefoot, I gave myself some rope sandals like the priests wore. My tunic was a doeskin brown, and I had a long brown scarf to wear over my head and shoulders. It was all a little shabby. I was indentured after all. Nothing I owned was mine. It was probably handed down from other slaves. At least it was all clean.

Around my neck on a leather thong was the talisman Lou had left me. It was invisible under the neck-high tunic and scarf. I unbolted the door with a soft thud and shut it quietly. I bolted the door from the outside with *energia* and walked down to the dining hall.

I did not see Craig but didn't want to. This meeting must contain no surprises. The truth was, I wanted it under my control. I needed to be strong and heartless. I would stop this infatuation of Craig's. Milly's kitchen was where I headed. Bernadette had yet to meet Milly. She was there, busy putting food on plates. The serving girl was waiting nearby. She paused for a moment as I walked in.

Peering at me in mid-spoonful Milly said, "You must be the lady's niece, Bernadette. Give me a moment to make ready these plates."

I nodded, not looking at her. I pretended to be shy. She loaded the plates and gave two to the serving girl, and she carried three, one plate balancing on her ample arm and one in each hand.

Milly came right up to me when she returned. She looked at my face and in my eyes. I thought she would look in my nose and also my ears if she could. Then she would open my mouth with both hands and check my teeth, just like a horse trader might if he were buying a horse.

"Ye be a pretty girl and healthy too, I'll wager. But can ye cook, sew, and keep a clean house? Ye be a might small to do much heavy work like might be needed on a farm. Speak up girl if ya be wantin' our Sir Craig. We need to know ya a bit." She put her hands on her wide hips and puffed up, bending toward me like a fox following its prey.

"I ne'r said I be wantin' Sir Craig, madam. Me aunt wanted me to talk to the man. Seems we 'ave met afore. Don't go gettin' all fidgety. Is he yer son?" I looked at her out of the corner of my eye with my head up.

That loosed her air a bit. She didn't expect me to speak, thinking I was a shy country girl. I wanted her to think that, but I could not help being honest.

"Ah, no. Well then," she fluttered.

The girl returned with dirty plates. She went right through, and I could hear her scraping them with a knife as she loosened the bits into the pig bucket on the back porch.

"Well, well!" Milly said again. "It be good ye can speak. Craig'll 'ave somethin' to hear."

She sat me at a corner table that was well lit. Craig would have to sit with his back to the room, all the better to discourage others from noticing him. I was covered from head to foot, and fortunately autumn was in the air, and it was cool.

When he walked in, he stopped in front of the doorway a moment. There weren't many taking supper right then, and he spotted me right away. I feigned not to recognize him. But I looked. He smiled and gave a little nod. So I bowed my head slightly. He was to go get Milly before approaching me. He strode through the room, a tall and confident man, comfortable with himself and his place. I could not help admire him. He was comely in a rough-hewn way. He would be a good husband. I was not his proper wife.

Milly came marching out of the kitchen with Craig following close behind, his smile still planted on his lips. "Here she be, Craig. This be Lady Fergus's niece, Bernadette MacTigue. I be yer guardian, but I know ye be the knight ye are. Shall I bring ye somethin'?"

"Do ye 'ave any o' that French wine left?" he asked before sitting. "If ya do, I will have two glasses, if ya please." He never took his eyes off me while he spoke.

Milly didn't answer, noticing his gaze, but turned and went back to the kitchen. He stood in front of me and reached out as if to take my hand. This was not allowed, but I couldn't refuse. I had only a moment to realize I needed a working girl's hand. Perhaps he was checking my story. I quickly created an illusion of calluses and cracks. They were not too creased and dry, but enough. It was what he expected when I placed my hand in his. He looked it over briefly and then lowered his head to kiss it. This surely was not allowed! I had a fleeting urge to recoil in surprise, but I didn't. I let his warm lips touch my cold wrist.

While he held me, I said in a quiet, childlike voice, "You are taking advantage of me, sir. Please release me."

He let loose my hand, just as Milly came bustling out the kitchen door with two full cups of wine. She reached our table and said in a loud voice, "This is special. Craig, ya haven't sat yet. Make yerself comfortable. 'Ere's yer wine. Enjoy!"

She pulled the chair out for him, and when he sat, she patted his shoulder like she was patting her favorite hound. Then back to the kitchen she ran as a large group of men came in the door.

"T'was only a couple weeks since we made our acquaintance."

I blurted out, "At least three weeks, sir."

"Three weeks, has it? Well now, time does fly like an arrow." He took a large gulp of his wine, draining half the glass. "Since that day when I fell off me horse, Curly, and you healed me of a grievous wound, one I reckoned would kill me, I 'ave been wantin' to meet ya again."

"I do not know why. Anyone would ha' helped a knight in distress." I shrugged my shoulders and followed up with a large gulp of wine myself.

"It was like an answered prayer when your aunt came to the jail ..." he began.

"I have na' got all that story," I cried. "She be accused of witchery." I lowered my voice. "And not even in town a day! What is happenin' in this town? I can't fathom it. She not even related to me own poor mum who was accused by a jealous woman with the men believen'. My mum had not a chance. And then she be taken and beaten by the sheriff, left to die in the hole!" My tears came quite without guile. I was reliving the whole scene. Before me was the son of the murderer.

"Kathryn be acquitted of all wrongs. It was a matter of bein' strange and in the wrong place. It is all over. I dare to say that she and me are on friendly terms. The sheriff was here and was rude to her. I canna' deny that. Sometimes it happens that way fer sure, but she be free." He sat back in his chair with a worried look on his face. This was not going as he expected it to.

We both reached for our cups. He drained his in one gulp. I took a less aggressive drink. He looked about for the server and yelled, "More drink!"

Milly must have heard because she came shooting out of the kitchen like an arrow loosed on its mark, carrying the pitcher of wine. She took one look at Craig and another at me. I was still leaning forward with a look of challenge on my tear-stained face. This kept her silent. She filled his cup and left the pitcher on our table.

I manifested a square of material from the pocket of my tunic and dried my eyes and face.

"I am sorry for yer mum, Bernadette. I ha' no belief in witches. Only common evil of the most vile sort can cause a person to die of witchery. Usually it is the accuser of the witch, not the witch herself, who is the evil one. Women accused of witchery usually have something the accuser wants." He sat in his chair with sagging shoulders.

"Truth," I said and took a drink. "Now me aunt is sick in her room. No doubt from cold nights in a cold cell. All she wants to do is leave. And I have onla just met her."

"And all I want to do is see yer face, Bernadette." He sat up, refreshed. "I want to tell ya that I want to marry ya. I 'ave loved ya since I first saw yer face through a fevered haze at the pond. Me horse must a liked ya too, or he would never ha' let ya get near."

He leaned his elbows on the table, just as Milly appeared with a small loaf of warm bread and a piece of cheese. She took a big breath as if to speak, but looking at Craig and the serious cast of his face, she once again retired quickly to the kitchen.

I could not hide my shock at the freshness of Craig's proposal. I did not expect it. This conversation was not under control. I felt very small. If I tried, I might be able to melt into the bench I was sitting on and disappear. If I could only find the *energia* of the thing I would be gone, just a pile of clothes would be remaining. Being anywhere else right now would be better than here.

No doubt in the back of my mind I had thought this might happen. I had storied myself to sleep at night with tales of a crofter life with Sir Knight. But I could not let him take me from my revenge, no matter who he was nor how much I might want him. The truth was that I would be inclined to say yes, if I were not who I was.

"I know this is quick. You had no knowin' of me afore this, and I was only a wounded knight who you helped without thought. Now I see ya again, and I know I want ya. I want ya for me wife. Ye were made fer me. That's all I can say. I dona' expect ya to say yes now, but I would want a further meetin' so we might become friends. Ya know nothin' about me or me family or who I am as a knight or gaoler for the sheriff. That job be only temporary, by the way. I have hope that yer aunt might say a good word or two of me and that you and me may 'ave another meetin'. What say ye, Bernadette?"

"Sir Knight, do ya know that I am but a slave? Much below yerself." I pointed this out, and I could hear my voice shaking.

"I heard from yer aunt yer indentured. That be a form of slavery fer sure. You must buy everything you need from the owner of your service, which means you owe him sometimes more than your pay. You may never be released from his service. That be the truth of it."

"Yes, but I can sew my own clothes from his cast-outs, and I don't eat much. I 'ave saved a small amount. I may be able to release myself by the time I am thirty. Then I will be too old for marriage."

"That be a long time away. I may be daid by then. I can't wait that long, but I will if I 'ave to." Then he leaned even closer, looking me full in the face. "Bernadette, I don't care how ye became indentured. I will buy yer contract and set ye free, whether ye marry me or not."

"Oh no, my lord. I would starve. I must work, or I will die. My owner is not unkind. I 'ave a warm and dry room, and he leaves me alone. I do me work as well as I can, and generally all is well. Without it, what would I be? I prefer you not knowin' where I be fer now."

"So yer aunt tells me." He slumped back on his seat once again. "Very well, my little love, I pine for you, and off you go. May we plan another meeting? I would not go without knowin' I could see ya again."

"I would have me aunt's advice, if ya please, sir. I will talk to her tonight, and she will give ya my answer. Ye be a comely man fer sure, and that be why I say to ya: do not wait for me. I have no thought to marry, and I am not inclined to change right now."

With that, I stood up to go. He also stood. I saw his long face drawn in sadness. I could hardly stand it. I wanted to touch him with comfort of some sort.

He reached for my hand again. Just an open hand he offered. It could not hurt to place my own hand there, so I did. He slowly brought it up to his chest and placed my hand over his heart, a place I had seen before: a wounded shoulder and torn shirt and my hand on his chest as he breathed slowly in and out. I felt the beating of his heart.

I drew my hand away. I could not look into his face as I turned to walk away. He must not detect any trace of a love for him I could feel welling up from the locked recesses of my own heart. I must push it away.

19

A JOURNEY

I walked into Milly's kitchen, accompanied by the air of an early-morning stroll in the gray, damp chill of a new autumn morn. I went right over to the huge fireplace that was crackling with its welcoming fire and the boiling teapot that hung over it.

"'Ave yaself a cup o' tea, missus, and tell me where ya been. Yer lookin' healthy agin fer sure." Milly was preoccupied with stirring a batter, perhaps for her famous bread.

"Yes, it was your mum's healing herbal I'm sure. I just walked my niece to the edge of town for her leaving. She must return to her work." I poured some tea into a large cup. "I am feeling much revived."

"The honey is there." She pointed with a flour-covered hand and then took the tough brown dough out of the bowl and started to knead it on a wooden board.

I watched her plump arms and hands as they worked the dough, and

I was envious. A life of making bread and food and taking care of people was a perfect life to my mind. Milly had it all. I admired her for it.

"And what o' yer niece, lady?" Her head was bent to her work, pushing and folding the dough. "What did she think o' our Craig now? A fine catch that one."

"True, a fine catch," I replied a little too dreamily. But Milly wasn't hearing subtleties. "Ah, but my niece has a mind of her own. She's not against a second meeting, but she will pick the time and place. In truth, I think it will be a long time coming. She's very young, even though she is sixteen years old. She has no sense of timing. She does not sense the months passing. It means nothing to her. Growing up without her mum has taught her hard lessons about doing for herself."

"Them be hard lessons." Milly agreed, looking up at me. "But Craig is a one who would take care in all ways. Will she be comin' into town? 'Ave 'er come to me. I'll give her a good meal and a talkin' to."

I finished the bottom of my sweet tea. "I did tell her to come to you when she was in town. Thank you, Milly." I put the cup on the board and started to walk out, but stopped. "By the by, you would not know of a cart I might hire to St. Andrews now, would you? I've a mind to go to a bigger town, and it is closer to Edinburgh."

"I think I can help ye wit that sure. When would ya be leavin'?" She put the loaf of dough in a bowl and covered it with a cloth.

"As soon as possible," I replied. "My stay here lacked a welcoming feel. I do want you to know I feel a friend in you and also in Craig. But I want to go back to my own familiar place. If that sheriff returns, don't tell him I said so."

"Don' you worry about him. And I'll be sorry to see ya go and hopeful ye'll come again." She wiped her hands on her grimy apron.

"I'll make some queries and find ya a trusty cart. It must be a five- or six-day drive at least."

"Yes, thank you, Milly. I'll be in my room."

I did not see Craig the next morning when I left in the horse and cart for St. Andrews. The driver was a small and lean older man, very much like the image Murray conjured for himself. The cart was a long-distance variety. It had leather straps that helped when going over the bumps in the road. They kept the inside of the cart from jouncing too much; the padded seat also helped. Unfortunately the swaying motion of the cab caused me to be ill.

"It's vera normal, madam," the driver assured me. "You'll get used to it fer sure. Less than a day. Yes, less than a day."

I tried to believe him as I was emptying my stomach out the side of the cart. I just wanted to lie down. The driver indulged my need for fresh air by not sealing the cab with the bright red cover. The first day was horrific, cold, and drizzly. Often the wind would blow water into my small sick room, and there was little I could do to keep dry.

We stopped at a farmer's croft the first night. They were accustomed to housing travelers that might come down their road. I had made a new letter of introduction with the stamp and sign of the bishop of St. Andrews, just to stick to my original story. Very few people could read, but the stamp looked official.

I was not a happy boarder, being wet and sick, but the farm wife had a room, and I paid her well to keep it for myself. I retreated to it as soon as I could. The driver would find a spot in the barn. I bought his dinner and his drink.

The next morning before the sun, I was back in the swaying cart. I had a small cloth wrapper of cheese and crusty peasant bread, which I gave to the driver. I was immediately ill from the bouncing and jerking of the conveyance. Sitting in that small, swaying vehicle day after day was no small feat. I sorely needed to get up and walk, but my stomach felt like it had small animals in it, clamoring to get out. I ate very little. There was a constant buzzing in my ears. I wondered if I might die right there in that awful cart.

Four days pass slowly when one is ill. We were nearing St. Andrews, and finally I noticed a moment of health. It came upon me so gradually that I hardly noticed that I was feeling normal. The sun was out, the birds were singing, the wagon was bumping, and I realized I had conquered the cart. I laughed out loud.

"I'm cured," I told the driver with a smile. "I do not feel sick."

"Well, it be about time," he said as he turned his head to peer at me over his shoulder. He turned back and clucked at the horse, who chose that moment to snatch at some grass on the edge of the track. "Four days was the longest I ever saw. I be thinkin' now ye be cured fer good. We be nearin' St. Andrews. 'Ave ya a lodging in mind, lady?"

"No, but might there be one ye know on the other end of town? I will be leaving for Edinburgh tomorrow."

"Aye, I know o' one. It be me own cottage, if it pleases ya. Me good wife be a fine cook and neat and clean as a whistle."

"I require a private room, sir. Is that possible?" I was not sure he earned enough to have acquired more than a hovel.

"Oh aye, me wife takes in sewin' and mendin', and our daughters help around the place. It'll cost ya, but no more'n wot ya already paid. An' I'll be 'ome wit me feet up and a whiskey in me." He nodded his head up and down and flicked the reins slightly.

"How long have you been out?" I asked.

"I do the Inverness run. It's six days out and six back, barring any bad luck on the road. And if I can get the riders quickly."

"Well, I am happy to stay for cleanliness and a good meal. I am growing very hungry."

"Right," he said, "off to Mrs. MacMurry's house. I be Mr. MacMurry, thank you."

"Now then, Mr. MacMurry, I will be needing to acquire transport on the morrow for Edinburgh. Can we make that ready today?"

"Of course," he said, flicking the reins again. "I have just the driver. Never ye fear, Lady."

St. Andrews was the largest city I had ever been in. Even late in the day, there was a bustling high energy to rival any chaos that might be found in Forresgem. The smell was completely given over to fish. It was a smell, strongly of the sea and the salt with rotting fish flesh sweetly intermixed. The fishmongers yelled their wares, dropping prices as we rolled by. It was too late in the day to expect fresh fish. Perhaps fermented fish would be a deal.

Some of the sellers were packing their wares. A candle merchant caught my eye, but I was not interested in buying. Looking and smelling were interesting enough after almost five days of being ill in the jouncing cart with leather straps that weren't much good.

We continued past the market street and turned onto a narrow lane between tall stone and wood buildings. There was no space between them. Like a castle, they were impressive in their stature. Not many people were out and about here. Very soon the buildings became single-floor hovels, some of them with only a ragged cloth over their doors.

Here, a more human stench filled my nose. The poor lived more closely together, many in nothing more than a couple wooden planks with a cloth overhead. I had never seen this level of poverty in Forresgem. As the hovels stopped and the ground opened up, the road became only wheel ruts in the grassy green. The heather of the hills beyond, in full purple bloom, gave the impression that all the world was purple starting just over there. As the sun set, we pulled up to a neat, white cottage with a thatched roof and a small attached barn.

"This be 'ome, and welcome to it, Missus Fergus." My driver limberly jumped to the ground and yelled, "Missus MacMurry, yer 'usband be 'ome. Come out!" He was not unfriendly. He eagerly helped me out of the cart with a hand.

The sturdy wooden door swung open, and out came a middle-aged farm woman, not plump but not thin and clean but slightly tattered with a tanned face and rosy cheeks. A white shawl was pulled over her head.

"Ah, Father, ye be back. And wit a boarder fer the night, me thinks." She came right up to me. Looking in the cart, she said, "A woman alone? An uncommon sight fer sure. Please be safe and welcome in our home. A bed and dinner for six bawbee is all we ask."

"I definitely require a bed, but do you have a whole room please? Name your price." I could see her calculating in her head.

"Hmmm. The room has three beds, and I usually 'ave three to each bed at seven bawbee per bed. That's twenty-one bawbee per room. But I have no boarders now, and it grows late. I'll give ya the room for twelve bawb and dinner for three more. That be fifteen total."

"Agreed, if the bed is clean," I told her.

"Oh yes, mum, clean covers this day. Straw but a week old I can fluff the mattress so it is as good as new."

"Very well, thank you. Might I go rest now?"

"Yes, lady, of course. I'll show ya the way." She rushed to open the door and held it for me. I collected the small bag of my personal things and followed her to the back of the house as the mister moved off with the horse and jouncy cart.

I did not remember having a meal. I was so tired that I just barely got into the bed before sleep overcame me. I awoke to a cock crow in the darkness before sun up, and a voice at my door called me to come. My travelling cart had arrived. I thanked myself for the magic I knew and, quickly righting my appearance, went to the kitchen.

The missus, already bright-eyed and busy, gave me a cloth with fried eggs between two pieces of bread and dripping butter. I thanked her and went to the cart, where it stood in the darkness before the day, a cloudy, cool day it would be too.

I magicked a thin shawl out of my wee bag, and wrapping it around my shoulders, I turned my wimple into thicker wool without anyone noticing. The driver was nowhere to be seen. I climbed into the cart anyway. It was a much more comfortable place than the other carts I had been in. The horse drawing it was as white as new-fallen snow, and I relaxed into its cushions, confident that I would suffer no illness.

The driver appeared from the kitchen. He was bundled up and took no notice of me. He was agile and lean, much younger than the other driver. As soon as he sat, the horse moved forward with a quick and jaunty step, as if it were looking forward to this trip. I could not see that the driver held no reins in his hands.

It soon became truth that he held no reins because it was Cullan and his white charger from the domain of the Slig Maith.

"Well, me lass, what 'ave you been up to these days? I have missed you."

I could feel his smile from the back of his head, and I was annoyed. I also marveled at the smoothness of the cart, its deep blue cover, and the beauty and agility of his elegant white steed. *Where is my black?*

I was sharp. "I have been seeking my revenge." I sat up, stiff-backed, despite the cushion's invitation to lounge. "I have had some success, you may know."

"We marvel at your skill. You 'ave not killed a single one of your tormentors, and yet one is dead, and another has been driven crazy. Why don't you just murder them with your magic and go on to the next? You dawdle here and there and take frivolous long trips to include time spent in gaol. Me mum would 'ave ya safely under her wing, doing her bidding as you 'ave promised."

He almost turned completely around in his seat but thought better of it because we weren't out of view of any crofter who might be out early. "And so would I," he added almost too low to hear.

I ignored it. "I wondered what happened to the sheriff," I said in a quiet voice. So that was it. He ran off without his mind. That would be a harsh life and a quick death.

"Did you not know?" Cullan asked with a laugh. "He has been running wild on the road to Edinburgh, seeking God and repentance for his crimes."

"That is just exactly what I would expect and want." I felt some satisfaction that he was running wild. "Seeking repentance is crazy?"

"It is, if he expects God to forgive him. He may find forgiveness among men. Then what good is your revenge? He will be comfortable and rewarded for his depravities."

He was right. Any sense of accomplishment I had vanished. The sheriff would find great relief with his fellows of the kirk. He would soon be acting on his evil intentions again. I had utterly failed. This knowledge fueled my anger.

"I'll find him in Edinburgh," I growled. "He can't get forgiveness while I'm around."

I was furious, not just at my inabilities but at Cullan's meddling. If my eyes had been weapons, they would have pierced the back of his head.

"What are you here for?"

He seemed to feel the attack in my voice and stiffened. "I'm here to drive you to the city. I'm here to take a look at you, to feel you near. I told you I want you by my side. I need to see you." His voice was soft and desperate.

I refused to believe him.

We drove for a long time in silence. Drawn by the miraculous white horse from a magical realm, the cart moved so fast and smoothly that I had to look to make sure we were still on the ground. My mind was in a haze of confusion. Here was Cullan, a prince. I never thought I'd see him again since his feelings for me could only be play acting. I could not possibly believe a son of a Slig Maith queen would fall in love with me. Craig was a man much more suitable for my likes. *But how could I ever think to be wife to him when I am a thing that would only frighten him?*

"The Slig Maith has chosen the wrong champion," I said, completely without thought. It had been vying for release in my mind, but I did not mean to say it out loud. My mouth produced it all on its own. "My magic is inferior, and my heart isn't into killing. I will do what I have to do for my mum's memory, but to helping the Good People, no, I would be a failure. And I sense the anger in your queen. She will kill me for my failure."

Cullan didn't answer. Maybe he was as shocked as I was to hear these thoughts. I had barely thought them, certainly not enough to bring them to voice. And yet there was the truth I had not admitted to myself.

We travelled along as far apart as strangers. The clippity-clop of the magic horse was like music. It might as well have been some strange and fanciful dirge for the darkness that gripped me on that cloud-covered, drizzly day. The sheriff needed attending to. I wanted to be done with him.

It was late afternoon, almost time to stop for the night. The sky was an angry gray with rain eminent for sure, and I was "stewing in my own juices," as my mum used to say.

"I am wanting to get to the barge at Kincardine. There's a friend in Grangemouth awaitin' on us," Cullan said. It was so matter-of-fact. Perhaps he had not heard me. Maybe he gave my declaration no importance. The cart took a slight lurch as the horse broke his smooth trot into a casual canter. So far we had avoided any settlement and only passed through farmland and forest, seeing very few people. There was a glamour on our cart, of which I could not tell. Only that it was there. I saw the truth; others saw what they wanted to see.

All day, we had brief views of the Firth. We tended to stay off the busiest roads along the coast, staying slightly inland. It was the most direct route from St. Andrews. Rather than go all the way up river to Stirling, we'd take a ferry barge across a narrow portion of the inlet to the bay.

We were nearing the small ferry when Cullan turned and asked me to pull the cover down over the cart. He said it would be more common a sight and would attract the least amount of attention. I felt for the handle with my mind and felt my energy go out to it, merge, and pull. Cullan was surprised at first, but as the bright blue cover with gold trim came down, he turned to look at me. I gave a small wave of my hand, and he burst out laughing.

"Brilliant!" he yelled.

I felt smug. I didn't know much about magic for sure, but I had learned a thing or two.

The ferry was just loading its last load of the day when we arrived.

"Ye can no' bring yer horse and cart on now, driver. We ha' no more room," a man said. Since I could not see, I only assumed he was talking to Cullan. "We start again at first light. Come back then."

Cullan was up to something. I could feel a small ripple of magic flow out. Immediately there came a "Haloo!" from the boat. I heard some confused yelling, and I could hear the ticket man, with Cullan beside him, walk quickly toward the water's edge. Some discussion followed, which I could not understand. But shuffling and scuffing on the flat wooden boat reached my ears. I looked around for a flap to open or someway to look out. There was none. In my frustration, I created one. It was very close to dark. No one would notice.

Men were moving boxes and barrels off the barge. Cullan stood talking to two men off to the side. One walked away abruptly. The other took something from Cullan, who turned away and walked toward me.

"Better close up that peephole afore someone sees," he said.

I could feel a little pitch in the cart as he got in his seat. I sealed the opening. "What have you done?" I asked quietly.

"Just created space," he said as the cart started moving down the slope to the ferry.

The white walked onto the barge with loud, hollow steps, and the cart jolted sharply as it was pulled on board. I could hear the water of the firth slapping against the boat's planks.

"All on board!" a man yelled.

"Is the light lit?" someone called.

"Aye, she be," another answered.

"Help with a shove, mates."

I heard splashing as some men jumped into the water. The boat seemed to shake and rise up. And then with a push and a tug, the ferry lurched forward as the rope on the other side got purchase, and I could feel the boat get caught by the current, going out it seemed. Men were grunting, and as they jumped back on board, the boat gave a little bounce.

Cullan was standing beside the cart. "Just pray the rope does not break, nor the men pulling flounder. The current is swift here. Can you swim?" I could feel a smile on his face.

"Of course," I lied. I had never been in water over my knees, except the tub in the Slig Maith tree house.

Since it had turned dark, I did not mind much not being able to see. I would not choose to be cooped up worse than a chicken in a pen like I was in that cart, but women of higher standing travelled this way. I could not figure if it were for their safety or the safety of anyone who might look in and lose his balance due to shock or some such idiocy. I would be on a horse out in the air like the men. I decided that this would be my last trip closed up in a cart.

Our crossing went without incident, and landing the boat was just a matter of pulling it onto shore. I could see torches flickering through the thin walls of my container. The air was moist and cool, and small waves lapped against the shore. The men moved the goods off the barge, and finally the cart started with a jolt.

"Hold on tight," Cullan said. "There's a drop off the boat."

I wasn't sure what to hold onto, but I braced myself for a pitch forward and a heavy drop as the wheels fell off the edge and into the rocky sand. Cullan's horse, Whitey (as I had taken to calling him in my mind), trotted up the slope and soon made a left turn onto a dirt road or path. We were moving along at a good speed so I raised the material of the cart.

"Won't be long now. Are ye hungry?"

It was a black night. The clouds had not dropped their water yet, but it seemed inevitable to me.

"No, not much," I replied. "This is like driving in a cave with no end. How can ye see?"

"My white can see vera well, so we trust him. I can also see. No night vision fer you?"

Just then I remembered my light, and it began to glow. I could see my hands and things that were close, but it wasn't enough to illuminate the outdoors. "No. Is it magic? Mayhaps I can learn."

"Me thinks it is a Slig Maith skill. We can walk in the day or the darkest night. It is all the same to me. But you are clever. Maybe you can coax that light brighter."

"You can see it?"

"Oh, aye, but it is yer magic. No human can see it."

The extreme dark made the ride seem much longer, but soon Whitey was turning onto a path that led to a sturdy stone house with shuttered windows and lights glowing through the slats.

Cullan had Whitey out of the cart almost before I had gotten down from it. I tucked my shawl around my shoulders a little more snugly. It was getting cold. The first drop of rain hit the top of my head, reminding me to cover my head.

Cullan looked at me in the dark and said, "No need to be coverin' yerself like a fearful human here, my missy. This be Donal's house, and he be Slig Maith, as free as the night."

I put the wimple over myself anyway. I was a human, and I was fond of being covered, except in a cart.

20

IN THE DARK

Cullan had let Whitey out of his traces and was releasing him beyond a corner of the house where he could graze, but the scrunching of gravel underfoot told me he was walking toward the door. He hadn't taken three steps when I could feel a wrongness. I didn't have time to call out, only to react. All my senses came to play, and I felt a blow coming, a powerful punch to my back just below my ribs, a very vulnerable place for the organs that lie there.

I swept my arms around, turning into my attacker like a whirling, spinning wind. His punch glanced off me. As I spun, my leg swept around, and I gave him a blow in his strong upper thigh. Lou had shown me a point there that would cause quite a lot of pain. It knocked him off balance for a moment. Simultaneously I circled my hands together and gathered energy, like a child offering a fruit. With both hands, I drove stabbing fingers into the throat of a man losing his balance.

I did not need to see my opponent. I did not need to see Cullan standing ready to throw magic at the man. The whole scene was unfolding in a slow, out-of-time motion. I did not see the man as a man, only as a life force, and I felt it through my body more than with my senses. He became me; I became him. He thought, for an instant, what an easy target I was. He would control me with one blow.

As he fell, he knew he'd been tricked and was now going to die. I knew I would not stop myself this time. I had learned my lesson, and I was not sparring with a worthy opponent. It was not Lou behind that solid fist. At the moment of impact, my fingers pointing like a metal blade to his throat, the door of the croft opened. Light flooded out from a bright fire on a burning brand. Cullan threw his magic.

My fingers seemed to brush the man's throat. Before it was over, I managed to hit him with another thunderous blow to his upper stomach, releasing lightning bolts of power. He gasped for air, but his collapsed throat inhibited his breath. I felt the life force leaving his body from his punctured throat as soon as he hit the ground. Mayhaps Cullan's magic did the final kill.

A blazing light flared out of the open door. The flickering brand lit the man standing there. Cullan stood in front of him, staring at me, with his arms outstretched from throwing the magic. The silence of the night roared in as we three stood there. The dead man was a Slig Maith.

"Donal! What is this?" Cullan yelled at the man in the doorway as he gathered his wits. "How dare ye attack Bernadette afore we even arrive! You must explain this, lad! We dare not enter til ye tell me, and even then, we dare not enter."

Cullan was afire with his own elfin glow. His whole body was alight with flames of magic, and he was ready for a fight. I felt calm. I was immune to their magic. They would have to fight me hand-to-hand. I had never taken on more than one, but Lou had trained me to take on eight. It was our style of fighting.

I mentally surveyed the area around the house and found no one hiding and no weapons raised. Whitey was blowing air out in loud snorts, standing by his master and friend, ready to fight if need be. Donal's energy prickled from the doorway.

"He's no one o' us," he said. "Be calmed, Cullan. Maybe one o' yer mum's?" He sent a large wad of spittle in the direction of the dead man. "I spit on his dust. We shall send 'im 'ome on the morrow and see what yer queen has to say then."

He looked up at me with wide and curious eyes. "My god, man, wot a woman ye got there! Please do na' stay out here. Ye be about to get wet, and I want to meet this human child who just laid low an almost immortal with two blows."

I walked around the body as the first drops fell, and into the bright warmth of the croft, I released my glamour and resumed my own appearance. Mrs. Fergus would be put away until needed.

"Willa!" Donal called in a booming voice. He was a big and broad man with shoulder-length, dark wavy hair and a chin full of black beard, someone I would label "woodsman" if I saw him in Forresgem.

"I hear ye, husband. Tea is ready whenever you are. I am here." A very small, very blond, young woman joined Donal in the middle of the room.

"Please, come be warmed and dry by our hearth. Be welcome to our board and relaxed in our company," she said. "I am Willa." She dipped in a small curtsy and tipped her head. "If you please," she added, conscientiously looking up at her bulk of a husband. She was not Slig Maith.

"Bernadette," I introduced myself.

Cullan was just coming in the door, his anger and surprise still plain on his face.

"Cullan has told of you. It is our honor to have you in our home. Please." She moved away from Donal, who had encircled her in a large, bearlike arm. "Please sit and rest. I'll bring some refreshment. A meal can be had at any time, when we are ready."

We all found a place to sit. Cullan was reviving as Willa brought in hot tea and some cheese to nibble.

I looked at him. "What was that then?"

The men both seemed stunned. Cullan was pale and withdrawn.

I looked at him. "What was that then?"

"It be a bad sign," he said, rubbing his eyes with his hands.

Donal agreed. "It be a very bad sign, if yer mum knows we are 'ere and wot we be doin'."

"This attempt to harm Bernie is a grave indication that she does." Cullan looked up, and in his face was not just worry but a fierce look of challenge. "It could be a war is unavoidable."

"What exactly is it you are doing?" I was the bystander. My life was forfeit for unknown reasons.

As their silence and blank stares reached an uncomfortable level, I jumped up from my chair, stamped my feet on the wooden floor, and yelled, "What!"

It had the effect I intended, even to getting Whitey's attention out in the yard. There was a whinny. The two men jumped out of their private thoughts and began to talk.

"What we are doin' is what I told you about when I first saw you. This here is the anti- Queen's Council, or some of it. I told you there were two councils. The Unseeley Council, the one the queen listens to, believes that all humans are less than animals and must die or be enslaved before they ruin the balance between us." Cullan's voice was dry and dull.

"Yes, I remember. The second council believes there is enough time to teach the humans how to get along with the earth." I spoke slowly.

It seemed so long ago when I had last seen Cullan. I had not thought of his words until now. My own business seemed much more current. Saving the race did not occur to me to be an urgent thing. Yet, in the back of my mind, I realized that I really didn't want to know what the plans were.

"It seems we 'ave come to a point of reckoning. The trouble is," Cullan said, standing and walking toward the blazing hearth, "I have no thought for how to proceed. This is a blatant act of violence coming a little soon in the game. I thought she would let you finish yer revenge. You have not asked for anything more than that." He folded his arms and looked over at Donal. "Why would she kill Bernadette when she was so wantin' to use her?"

"Mayhaps the plan weren't to kill her, just to wound her and steal her to the queen? I do na' know." Donal ran his fingers through his beard. "How would the one man have gotten her away from us? Mayhaps thar's more out there?" He gazed toward a shuttered window, and we all turned our heads.

"I had no feeling of others in the yard. Wouldn't your white let you know, Cullan?" I asked.

"Aye, sure. If he knew. They could conceal themselves in their magic. But not from you. I didn't even know the one Maith was there til I saw you moving swiftly to put him down. You have a powerful magic fer sure. I have seen it twice and still can't believe it."

I did not see it as magic so much as a skill I had learned from Lou.

But maybe it has some magic in it? Certainly the using of elemental energy is a kind of magic.

"Mayhaps it was a single council member acting alone? Someone wanting to show the queen his loyalty?" Donal offered.

"It does not make a difference," Cullan mused, turning back to the hearth. "How to proceed? That is the question."

"You need to find out—" Donal began.

I interrupted. "Do not forget that I have my own concerns. I am not beholden to the queen, as our agreement was clear. The agreement was to finish training and complete revenge. Then I will think about what help I can give her." The latter wasn't exactly the agreement, but I was feeling powerful.

"Have you known her to go back on a promise?" I looked up at Cullan, who faced the hearth.

"Only with humans," he said. "Usually she tricks them into going against their best interests. Their downfall is usually greed. In your case, it was your own lust for revenge."

He was right. She had tricked me. I was who I was because of her.

He turned to look at me and saw the shock of the realization on my face. He smiled a sad smile. "She tricked you because of yer innate personal magic. You be a rare bird who can manage in both realms, and that is yer natural talent. Now she has turned you into a weapon. What will be yer target? You can choose."

Before I could answer, he went on. "I came to you to convince you to follow our council's beliefs. I know you have a revenge to fulfill, but I want ya to know you have a choice. You be stronger than the queen."

How could I possibly be stronger than the queen of the Slig Maith? She is naturally magical. My magic is sleight of hand compared to hers. Even if I want to believe him, how could I? I wasn't even sure the Seeley Council was actually against the queen.

There was an uncomfortable pause. "Can we eat now, wife?" Donal asked. "Me thinks our minds need nourishment and rest."

Donal and Cullan stayed in the kitchen late into the night, discussing what they should do. Donal no longer felt safe and wanted Willa to go into hiding. It seemed a proper plan to me. Their planning seemed not to concern me. They plotted where to organize and who to notify. I was so close to resuming my task that I had little interest in theirs.

I was forming plans of my own. I was shown a pallet on the floor next to the hearth, and I took my leave, feigning extreme tiredness. The men huddled together in the kitchen, trying to keep their voices low. The dark night deepened. It was still, and the moist air settled around everything.

"I must go out for relief," I called. "Only a moment."

"Watch yerself," Cullan hollered back.

I opened the door, and it creaked and snapped shut as I closed it. I waited, testing the local vicinity. I put a thought out for Ciaran. Then I opened the door as if going in. I called "good night" and shut the door.

No one answered, but I could hear the men in constant conversation. They heard me and assumed I was back inside. I had stuffed my pallet to make it look like a body covered in blankets was on it. I walked like air out into the late night where nothing moved, except Whitey, who moved in his sleep. He had one eye open. I sent him a feeling of comfort and rightness, "seeking relief, no worries." And I continued my silent, fluid walk out the gate and into the dripping woods beyond the house. Ciaran was waiting.

It was not the reunion I would have wanted. I flung my arms around his big neck, and he hung his heavy head on my shoulder.

"Trouble?" he asked. It was a clear question but a new language. His mind spoke to me, more in feelings and forms.

"Some trouble," I thought back. "I must flee. I have a job to do. Please come."

He seemed to understand. He softly blew air out his nose. "Whitey?"

"He sleeps. He will tell Cullan. Not good."

He gave his head a toss and knelt down until he was crouching on the ground. I quickly replaced my gown with leggings and climbed up. "To Edinburgh, dearest. As fast and as quiet as we can," I whispered.

21

REVENGE

Fortunately our journey to Edinburgh took place in the dark of a cloudy night. We met with not a single soul since Scotsmen were loath to be about at dark of night. Because of it, we stayed to the road rather than the woods, and we made good time, arriving on the outskirts of the town just before dawn. The castle loomed ahead, a dark mountain against the gray early morn.

"I cannot bring you into the town, my beauty. You would attract too much attention," I told Ciaran as I slid off his back, hitting the ground with a thud and leaning into his shoulder.

His warmth encompassed me with strength. The dark morning was cool, and he breathed out misty clouds. Frost was on the way.

"I will call you when I need you."

He tossed his head and shifted slightly as I stood back. "I wait," he said. "You hurry."

I stepped out onto a road called the Cow Gate. "Be safe," I called to him.

As I walked, I slowly changed my illusion, for that was truly all this body was, the sack that we carried with us to house what we were. We clothed it with our thoughts and attitudes, and we became what we thought we were. I liked being what I was, a sixteen-year-old girl, but that image was fraught with issues. I did not want to attract attention. Sixteen-year-old girls could not help attracting attention, and those travelling alone would be like a sweet pie to hordes of flies. I wanted to go into town unseen and come out unseen.

By the time the sun came up behind the clouds of that early morning, I was walking the Cow Gate in a ragged and stained smock, with a bent back loaded with firewood and in my hand a stick to help my walk. My hair was white and sticking out in unruly tangles from a tattered black scarf. My feet were bare, my hands were gnarled and bent, and my sun-browned face was etched in deep lines. I took out some teeth and squinted out of half-blind eyes.

In between the peeling of the bell from St. Giles Cathedral was the sound of mingling crowds of people. There were peasants in little more than rags and merchants dressed for business thronging around the Netherbow Port, the main entrance to the walled city of Edinburgh.

"It be free market day," I heard one merchant say. "That be why all the peasants come this way. The tolls be waived."

Pointing to the top of the wall, the other man said, "Seems a few new heads upon the heights. They've paid their final toll."

Along the high wall beside the gate were the severed heads of recently executed criminals. Since they were not removed very often, some of them were skeletons with smiling, gaping jaws. Three of them were fresh, two men and a woman.

"Do ye hear o' their crimes?" he asked his friend.

"No, probably stolt. Little news comes outside the wall," he replied.

I followed behind them closely as we neared the narrow entrance of the gate.

Just because it was free market day didn't mean there weren't guards. Each person was looked at and judged. But the line moved along. The two I was following seemed to know the guards, who asked about their families and waved them through. I sidled up to the gate, slowed, and eyed the guards through my feeble eyes.

"Hurry on through, Granny. Sell yer sticks and be gone afore dark or yer owin' a toll. Ya know it's comin' and goin'. This be land's end fer ya should ya miss the leavin' time today."

"I heard ya," I screeched. "I be bringin' this 'ere bundle to Janet MacTigue, ya know. But I cain't 'member whar she be?" I opened one eye wide and grimaced a toothless grin.

"Hey, Gwin!" The guard turned and yelled at a man standing inside the gate, "Ya know Janet, doncha? Whar she be?"

"Now ya be wantin' a piece o' her?" he yelled back with a laugh. "She be in the whorin' district. Don't rightly know the street. But ya kin ask anyone thar fer Janet. They'll know."

"I thought ye might 'ave an idea." He turned back to me. "Didja hear, Granny? Can ya find the whorin' district? Walk up High Street to Castle Hill. Ya can na' miss it."

"Aye, sir. I be goin' directly thar, surin' she can be usin' these sticks." I moved off, resettling my load and my bent back.

I was not surprised to hear where Janet was. Dougal must have quit her. A woman with no means of support would certainly end up in the whoring district.

I turned down a narrow street and was soon out of sight of the port.

It was still early morning. Not many people were out, but housewives were up and about, bed linens were hung out to air on balconies, and chamber pots were being emptied onto the cobbled street.

I had to watch where I put my bare feet, so I soon clothed them in shoes. The cobbles turned to dirt, the buildings turned to tenements, and as I walked, I dropped my sticks near the door of one such place and turned down another road, heading back toward High Street. I restored my body and replaced my clothes as I went; a plain shift, apron, and scarf. I could be a serving girl on a mission for a laird.

Back on High Street, merchants were opening their businesses. Young women just like myself were busy, perhaps shopping for their households. The butcher was doing a brisk trade, and I passed cobblers, tailors, and merchants who serviced the castle and court officials. Edinburgh was the seat of power for Scotland, and it felt big and rich.

I had to stop to stare at St. Giles Cathedral. I had never seen a cathedral before. Its gray stone mirrored the gray day, and its steeple hovered overhead, trying to pierce the covering clouds to let the sun in. If my kirk were as big as three seagoing ships, this was the size of twenty. Ponderous and immense up close, it got lighter as it reached the sky. I dared not go in for fear the tortured gods within might overwhelm me.

High Street became steeper, and I trudged along. The merchants here had walled and fenced properties. Perhaps these were the residences of nobles or castle attendants. The houses were set back a bit, and some had gardens. This was too nice an area for whores to be working. I turned down a side street and followed it around as it came up under the cliff below the castle and into a squalid settlement of stone structures with hide roofs. The smell of death and dying was everywhere. The street was constantly wet, some of it from chamber pots and from wet runoff from the castle grounds. Lack of sunlight did not help. Light was permanently avoiding this place. It must have been dark and gray, even on the sunny days. Here and there, a gray-faced woman looked out the door of her hovel.

I stopped in front of one of the hovels. A woman stood just outside. She was showing a pregnancy. Her round belly protruded from the filthy rags she wore. She crossed her arms and challenged me with her stare.

"Pardon me, please." I looked at the ground in front of me. "I wonder if ya could tell me of Janet. Does she live aroun' 'ere?" I looked up.

Her hardened, cross face softened a wee bit. "Aye, just two doors that way." She pointed her hand.

I curtsied with a bob and turned quickly to run away. Janet's house had a wooden door and a window with shutters.

I scratched on the door. "G'day, mum. May I enter?"

"Who be ye? No a man? I dona' see women. Try Glory down the walk." The voice was old and tired, and I detected pain.

What a shock! There were whores who saw women. I didn't have time to think about that.

"No!" I said a little too loudly. "I need to see Janet MacTigue from Forresgem."

"That be meself. Come in and state yer business then. And bring ample coin."

I pulled at a rope in the door, and it opened, flooding me with a dank odor of wet ground and the pungent flavor of wet, moldy hide. It was almost too much to breathe as it wrapped around me like a diseased blanket. After a couple breaths, I stepped in and felt my skin crawl. There was another odor in the air, the smell of rotting flesh.

"Close the door, girl, and be quick," Janet howled, and finishing the sentence, she fell to a gurgling, rasping cough that had her grabbing at her heart with a bony, old hand. When she could speak, she demanded, "Who sent ya 'ere? No' Craig fer sure. Who be ye?"

I had to brace myself for the truth. This old woman, only four years older than when I last saw her, was going to die. From what I could see from the meager light coming in under the hide roof, the beautiful Janet of my memory was now a sick, elderly hag.

She was sitting on a thin pallet with her back against the lichen-encrusted stone wall. Her feet splayed out in front of her, and her rags just barely covered her. Her toes were black, her fingers were too, and she had black, open sores on her arms and legs. Her face was lined and filthy. Her once-glorious blonde hair was now strands of dirty gray. Most curious were her eyes. They ran with water, and her cheeks were raw for the rubbing of them.

"Don stare!" she yelled.

I quickly turned my head.

"It be the stab of a witch I got. Now I be dyin' from the water elf disease."

"Oh really," I said, relieved of my compassion. "When did this happen to you?"

"It 'appened four years ago by that witch I set to the barrel."

Now I was angry. I looked her in her watering eyes, but she could just barely see. She had no knowing who I was.

"Did you put that on your list of complaints? Did the sheriff know you'd been stabbed when he was raping my mum? How 'bout Dougal? Did you tell him you'd been stabbed? When did he desert ya? Did Craig know you'd been stabbed?" I wanted to stab her again.

"How?" Her voice suddenly got soft. "How did ya know all them people? Ye say yer mum?"

I put my image to her mind. She suddenly recoiled. She held herself with her arms and pulled her knees to her chest.

"Ye be back ta finish me off!" she yelled.

"I am the daughter. I have come for my revenge. But I can see you have ruined your own life. My revenge is complete."

She began to cough in huge gagging bursts. Blood spewed from her mouth onto the dirt floor. I gave her body a kind of energetic look over. I had never done it before, but by desire only I saw that something, an animal was eating at her heart. With every pump of her blood, bits of this animal moved through her body, eating at her. It was a painful way to die, but not a plague.

"I did come to kill you," I said without emotion. "I have one question for you, and that is, where is Dougal?"

She gasped for breath. "He left me as soon as we came 'ere, and I 'ave no knowin' what road he took. I could na' go back to me husband, nor to the town where I be borned. All was lost, and now I 'ave lost meself." Water flowed from her eyes, and she sprawled helplessly in the filth and gore on the floor.

My compassion returned. I manifested a cup of clean water and offered it to her. She could not right herself so I went to her and held her reeking body in my arms. I put the cup to her lips. Her small, wasted body was just bones and skin, sores, and rottenness. I couldn't hold back my own tears. The door opened.

A tall man stood slouched in the low doorway. He peered cautiously into the dark, moldy room.

"Mum?" he said with a worried sound. He stepped in slowly and surveyed the filthy, nearly empty room.

"She is here, Craig," I told him. My voice wavered with my crying.

She and I sat on the diseased floor in front of him. As his eyes found us, she took a last rasping breath and died.

"My God, Bernadette! What be ye here fer? Me mum! What has become of her?" He fell to the floor on his knees in front of us.

To tell the truth or to make a lie? I was not sure which way to go. I wiped at my face with the edge of my scarf.

"I came to see your mum and my aunt. But your mum has died here in my arms. I am sorry."

He looked over his mum's body. "From the look o' her, she be vera sick. And you there tryin' to doctor her vile body with all the sores and the stink. Ye must be some kind o' angel from heaven." He looked down at his poor mum and stood up. "Here, come away from that body. It may be plague."

I stood and brushed at my apron and shift, now covered in filth and blood, "No, not plague. Some disease of the heart, I think."

I was not sure what to think about this third attempt at finding my revenge. I could not consider it a total failure since my foe was dead. But there was something that I could not deny. I still hadn't completed a single revenge murder, something I had dreamed about and thought about for so long that it never even occurred to me that I couldn't actually do the deed.

"Come away. I will make arrangements for burial. Have ye a room? Can ye clean yourself from the gore? Change clothes?" He had little care for the woman who had birthed him. Her body lay on the floor in a crumpled heap.

"I did not come to stay. It is free market day. I would leave tonight before the toll. I fear my aunt has moved on, and I have no idea where she would go."

"I can aid you, and we must talk. I have friends in Cannongate. Come with me, and we will go there now. On the way, I will notify the priests." He walked to the door and turned to me, holding out his hand. "Come."

22

WANTING

Craig notified the priest who would send grave diggers for Janet's body. He paid some money but was not interested in a funeral mass or burial in a sanctified graveyard. "Out in a field is good enough," he declared. She would have an unmarked grave in the poorest graveyard, outside the walls of the city.

I should have felt some triumph. Janet was dead. But my mind was troubled. This was not the way I was supposed to end my stay here. I was not wanting to be with Craig, nor to meet his friends. I was wanting to be alone, to be unknown, to be free. Instead I felt harnessed. I could not do what I wanted to do. How could I leave now? Craig was beside me and would not let me go. We walked out the Netherbow Port and straight down the dusty road toward the village of Cannongate.

He stopped and looked at me. He had such a glow in his eyes, and his face was so soft and tender. A look of love was all I could imagine. His comely features seemed more enhanced to my eyes, but it only increased the havoc of my mind. I frowned. I couldn't begin to think that I might love him. I needed to find the sheriff. I needed to finish what I was trying to do.

He drew me to him and held me to his chest, pressing my head to him like a mother and a child. Kissing the top of my head, he murmured, "I love thee, Bernadette MacTigue. Promise to be mine for all time and make me the happiest man to ever live. I will never fail to try to make you the happiest woman."

I did not struggle. Pressing against him gave me great comfort. What was this between us? I could love him. I had known this as truth, but the place I found myself in was not a place I could bring him. I was more Slig Maith than human.

My heart beat in time to his, and I only wanted to linger in his arms until time came to a halt, but I knew that people I loved could be in great danger from enemies who wanted to hurt me.

I pushed away. "I'm sorry, Craig. I have a past that puts me in danger. Please understand that, if I were free, I would try to love ..." I did not get the rest of the sentence out.

"Danger?" he asked, still in the thrall of his feelings. "How can that be? Ye are still so young. What have you done? I could help ya."

He did not believe me. I was tempted to tell him everything just to watch his face as understanding flooded in and he knew I was a "witch" with ties to the Good People. We stood, close together under a copse of wide, leafless trees. It was the only cover on the road we were following.

"I am afraid I am someone under a curse," I whispered.

"No!" he cried. "That can't be. You be too young."

"It's not quite a curse. Really, it's more like a bargain."

"A bargain? With who?" He looked at me with such an open, loving face that it hurt me to see.

I could have flung myself into his arms and asked him to take me away. But there was no away from the Slig Maith.

"Tell me," he said, once again enfolding me in his arms.

I wanted him to protect me. I almost believed he could. "Tis a long story, but it was a deal I made after my mum died with the Good People—"

"No! Not the Slig Maith!" He grabbed my shoulders for a moment.

Worry filled his eyes. He pulled me to him again, and this time, I held him. My eyes teared up, and my throat tightened.

"Yes," I whispered. "And they are coming now to take me away." I could feel Cullan and Whitey approaching. "But the one who is coming is a friend. He is taking me to hide for awhile."

"Where, my love? I wish to be by your side, no matter in this realm or the other." His voice was soft and confident, but the battle raging in his mind was clear to me.

"You must not let them know you love me! They will find you and hurt you. There is evil there. My loved ones are threatened."

The sound of horses galloping came down the road. We had to separate but not before Craig bent down and kissed me long and hard. Such sweetness I had never known; such desire for more I had never felt. It was a life-affirming kiss, one that shocked me to realize that I wanted to live.

Before, I had only revenge to keep me moving. Now I felt something more. For a kiss, for Craig, I could live. I held him tight for a moment more. As our bodies parted, I felt something lodge in my heart. It was he.

He was still holding my hand when Ciaran galloped up. Close behind were Whitey and Cullan.

"Ah! What have you been up to this day, my little vixen?" Cullan didn't dismount, better to command from a horse for sure.

Ciaran walked right to me with his nostrils flaring. He eyed me and sniffed. "Good?"

"Aye, very good," I said out loud. "Cullan, this is Craig, my friend from Forresgem."

"Craig." He nodded his head but his mine and eyes were all for me. We could not imagine you would leave our safety. What was on your mind, child?"

"I have seen to my business. Thank you." Craig had no idea his mum was my target.

"Well, well, I almost think ye be as dangerous as me mum suspects. I will ne'r question your purpose in the future. I cannot wait to hear the tellin' of it. But now we must go. Time is important. My friends have sent the murderer back to me mum. She'll be sendin' reinforcements soon, no doubt. We are leavin' Scotland." His gaze shifted to Craig, and I could see him taking measure of the man.

"Where be yer journey's end?" Craig demanded as he stepped up to Whitey.

He did not try to touch the horse or get close enough that a flashing hoof or tearing bite might reach him. He was a large and imposing man, a match for Cullan in a fight for sure.

"Do you know what danger ye be in, man? Did our little missy tell you who I be but the prince of the Slig Maith? It's me own mum we be runnin' from. If you know, you become a danger to us. I do not think you should know because then you also become a danger to yerself."

Whitey stomped a foot in warning.

"I am a knight and good in a fight. Let me travel with you. I can help." Desperation strained his voice.

"Do you have magic?" Cullan looked at Craig like a raven wanting to snatch a shiny bauble. "Our little missy does, ye know." He smiled a wicked grin. "I have seen her drop a man about your size twice now, and one was a Slig. That one she killt, she did not use normal magic for that. She is a skilled hand fighter with a kind of magic not known of. I can see by the look on yer face she had not told ye that part yet."

Craig turned to look at me with a mix of disbelief and fear. "Is this truth?"

"Aye, tis. I am trained to fight." I folded my hands and looked at my feet.

All was lost now. *Love is a fleeting feeling, just like illusion. Emotions come and go. They make us beautiful and ugly as well as happy and sad.* I let any love I had for Craig run off like a freed fawn looking for shelter.

Both horses had saddles and some kind of bridle with a rope but no bit, for appearances I knew. Slowly I turned to Ciaran. He would need to crouch for me to mount, even with the useless saddle. I stood looking at the stirrup, which was just at eye level. He went down, and I climbed on. I had to transform my dress into something less fitting. I did not care if Craig took offense. It was for the better. He could get on with his life.

I looked down at him from my black's back, already missing what I could not have. Craig was deeply hurt, his lips were tight, and his eyes were too wide and filled with water. Without a care for Ciaran, he came to me and reached up for my hand.

He brought it to his lips and whispered, "I have seen and known many things. I will find you. Only death can stop me."

Cullan said, "Good to meet ya, Craig. Don't wait up. Come now, Bernadette, to safety."

A raven croaked and snapped its wings in the tree above our heads. The horses whirled around, and we were off.

23

FLIGHT

I was fleeing from Craig more than I was fleeing with Cullan. There was no escaping the queen. I was sure she'd be waiting around every bend with an entourage of elvish knights mounted on their war beasts, bloody and snarling. *How could she kill her own son?* She was a hard and cruel person.

I wanted to flee. At least that was what I told myself. I shall never see Craig again for his own good. I was not the partner that would make his life better. I would only be trouble for him. Cullan believed he needed my help. Or perhaps he was lying. I had no trust in the Slig Maith. Even the queen had gone back on her word and tried to kill me before I had completed my revenge.

I couldn't look back. I knew Craig stood there, tense and confused, trying to figure out what to do. He could never follow us on our magical steeds. Ciaran and Whitey galloped over the road out of Edinburgh as if they were the winged horses of mythology. Their hooves didn't touch the ground. *What would Lou do?*

I made my body one with Ciaran. The gathering and spring of his muscles, his stretched-out neck, and flaring nostrils was me. Our stride elongated as we raced down the open road, the castle receding in the distance. As we bunched, coiled, and released our muscles, my mind became still, and I relaxed into the joy of being a horse running free. There was nothing to fear. There was no worry. There was no problem to solve right now. This was how I passed the day until we finally stopped at a clearing in a dense wood just off our path.

Ciaran and Whitey touched noses and arched their necks, blowing out great gusts of air. What fun indeed, to be so free to run forever. Ciaran let me know how happy he was to be with me.

I put my face in his mane and hugged his neck. "Thank you, my love," I told him.

I felt like I was in a dream. *How does this joyous feeling fit into the situation we are now in?* I could see that Cullan did not share it.

"We are a little early. We are meeting someone here momentarily," he said.

Whitey dropped his head to nibble some brilliant green grass at his feet. Cullan slid off his back. Before he could step over to me to help me down, I flung my leg over Ciaran's neck and slid gently to the ground. Stepping back to lean into his huge, warm body, I nestled into his shoulder, something that could become a habit. I closed my eyes and breathed in smells of fresh grass and horse breath. Ciaran smelled salty and comforting, like a warm croft and a loving family.

It was a fleeting moment, for I sensed other beings in the woods. Some were Slig; others were not. I need not say a thing as Cullan was aware of their approach also.

"This be our companions approaching," he stated. "Use your skill to feel their intent. If a one is not with us, you will tell this to me."

"Of course."

Need he ask me? If I had that skill, I would certainly warn him. But if I had it, I hadn't noticed that I did. I kept my doubts to myself since suddenly there were eight men standing in the clearing as if they had simply appeared from air.

As far as I could tell, there were three Slig Maith and five humans. They were similarly dressed in brown leggings and a shirt. Some had leather coats; others wore wool sweaters. They all had long blades at their hips and knives in their belts. A couple of the men had tattoos covering their faces, shaved heads, and necks. These wild eyed men were fierce and frightening.

One man's long face was turned into a raven, his nose being the jutting beak. I could see open talons partly exposed on his upper chest. It made me think the bird was reaching out to land or to grab at something. It was fascinating, and I could not stop staring at him, wondering about the rest of the tattoo and if I were right about its position.

The other man's tattoos were of something rarely seen. He was a dragon. At least that was what I saw. He had a serpent head with fangs that seemed to protrude from a hideous up-curved mouth. A forked tongue lolled down his chin to his neck. Scales covered his face and head, and his eyes were like dark recesses where glowing orbs hypnotized one to his death.

Cullan grasped the arm of one tall Slig. "Ru! My friend! Grand to see you!"

Ru clapped the prince hard on the shoulder. "Aye, my friend, my service is yours. And you know these others, Halvar and Mick."

The camaraderie of the three Slig Maith was obvious as they

pounded each other and grasped arms with friendly closeness. The human men gathered around the prince, eager for introduction. Only the two tattooed men hung back. I stayed tightly tucked into the loving shoulder of Ciaran as he munched. The only sign of tenseness he showed was the quick tug and loud chewing of his head.

"These men here be Brian, Niall, and Faolan. The best of the best and more to come when battle nears," Ru said. "We 'ave two others. In the shadows they be lurking."

The tattooed monster men stepped up. I could see the pride they felt as they swaggered toward the prince. The raven man grasped the prince's arm tightly.

Ru said, "This be Fiach Dubh. Call him Raven. This 'ere other be Oll Pheist. We call him Dragan."

The prince looked over the two men. "We thank you fer your service. How be the Emerald Isle of late?"

Raven answered, releasing his arm. "It be as bonny as ever was, and we look to our return with happiness. It is an honor to serve ye, Prince."

He made way, and Dragan stepped up. He tipped his head to the prince but did not speak nor reach out.

The prince responded, "Me thanks, Dragan."

These men were warriors of Ireland. I watched them closely as they stood relaxed and ready. I knew fighters when I saw them.

Just then, Ciaran took a step and practically threw me into the crowd of men.

I stumbled momentarily. "Eh-hem." I coughed lightly.

Cullan had seen the whole thing. Thank goodness he refrained from laughing. All the men turned. I saw shock first flash through their faces and then relaxation mixed with uncertainty. They didn't seem to know what to do. I was sure the human men had never seen a one such as me. The three Slig Maith had been warned.

"Do we not get an introduction?" Mick asked, turning to glance back at Cullan.

"This is Bernadette, of course."

"Bernadette, aye," said Ru. "Might we have a formal introduction, Cullan?"

"This be Ravenheart," Cullan began.

Some of the men gasped and mumbled.

"Your reputation precedes you," he continued with a laugh.

"But I have done nothing ..." I started.

Are they mocking me, as men often do to women? I stood my ground, planting my feet and drawing up the power of the earth. I relaxed down, firmly standing ready for anything.

"Because of you, we are here," said Fiach Dubh (Raven). "Your power is our only hope when the queen of the Slig Maith presses battle."

The men and the Slig, except Cullan, all dropped to their knees, with their right fists over their hearts.

Ru said, "We pledge to support you, Ravenheart, to the death if need be."

All the men yelled at once, "Aye, so be it!"

A large black raven with spiraling golden eyes dropped to the ground in front of me, screeching, "What! What! What!"

Printed and bound by PG in the USA